HELL ON WHEELS

Barry Rivers spat out the window, trying to get rid of the sudden bad taste in his mouth. He grimaced his disgust and distaste. Animals. Dangerous, rabid, maddened animals was what he could compare the Anson boys to. "Makes my job much easier," he finally spoke. There was a note of finality in his statement.

And Brenda knew then that there would be a lot more blood spilled in Dane County. A lot of it spilled by this man.

What she did not know was how much blood.

Buckets full.

Dear Friends,

I've had so many requests for the return of the RIG WARRIOR series that I've finally persuaded my publisher to bring them back. Here they are—one each month, in July, August, and September!

Barry Rivers has always been a favorite among the heroes I've created. Like many an independent thinker, Barry doesn't like to wait for the slow wheels of justice to turn, so he takes matters into his own hands. He travels alone—with his trusty partner, Dog, beside him in his eighteen-wheeler.

I hope you enjoy the RIG WARRIOR books. If you do—or even if you don't—I'd be happy to hear from you. You can write to me of my publisher, or e-mail me at dogcia@aol.com

Happy reading!
Bill Johnstone

RIG WARRIOR WHEELS OF DEATH

William W. Johnstone

Pinnacle Books
Kensington Publishing Corp.
http://www.pinnaclebooks.com

This novel is a work of fiction. Names, characters, places, and incidents are either the product of the author's imagination or are used fictitously, and any resemblance to actual persons, living or dead, or to events is entirely coincidental.

PINNACLE BOOKS are published by

Kensington Publishing Corp.
850 Third Avenue
New York, NY 10022

First Printing: April, 1988
First Pinnacle Printing: August 2000
10 9 8 7 6 5 4 3 2

Printed in the United States of America

Pale Ebenezer thought it wrong to fight,
But Roaring Bull (who killed him)
Thought it right!

Hilaire Belloc

The talent of a meat-packer, the morals of a money-changer, and the manners of an undertaker.

W.A. White

One

His natural birth took place in a New Orleans hospital. He was the son of a truck driver and a housewife. He was named Barry. His mother died when he was just a boy. He could barely remember her. He was Irish on his mother's side, Cajun French from his father.

Barry Rivers could drive an eighteen-wheeler by the time he was ten.

He graduated from high school at sixteen, went to college for a couple of years, and then, bored by it all, went into the army. He spent his time in Vietnam as captain of an A-Team, Special Forces. When he left active duty, he stayed in the Reserves while finishing his education and driving a rig part-time for his father. He got married, fathered two kids, and then was divorced, his wife taking the children and cloaking herself behind a wall of old Eastern money. By then, Barry was president of a consulting firm—civilian weapons expert for the Defense Department—and making a lot of money. No serious relationships since his ugly divorce; he didn't have time.

When he decided to go home to New Orleans for a short vacation and to see his father, Big Joe Rivers, he found his father in all sorts of trouble: mob trouble, it first appeared, but it turned out the two men behind it all were Barry's brother and Barry's own partner in business.

His brother eventually went insane. Barry, months later, killed his partner, Jack Morris.

Barry took a leave of absence from his company and took over Rivers Trucking. He didn't know that agents from the Treasury and Justice departments were setting him up for a fall.

But he'd survived bad falls before.

Barry had slipped back into trucking with ease. Then he met Kate Sherman. Tiny, blond, very pretty. One hell of a truck driver. Barry and Kate would marry.

Then a bomb planted in Barry's pickup truck, intended to kill him, killed Kate instead. The blast landed Barry in a hospital in New York State. He would lie in a coma for months. When he came out of it, he would learn he had been reborn.

Barry Rivers was officially listed as dead.

He had undergone many operations and much intensive therapy, mentally and physically. One side of his face had been completely reworked, altering his appearance. His smashed nose had been rebuilt and reshaped. The bomb had not killed him, but it had come close.

Barry learned that he was officially dead, buried beside his wife, Kate, in a New Orleans cemetery.

"You're dead, Mister Rivers," he was informed. "Your package has been pulled by Central Records. Your social security number retired. Your life insurance paid off. You no longer exist."

That took some getting used to. But Barry knew why it was happening to him.

He had met the President of the United States. Man was just as tough as he looked. "Country has gone to hell, Barry," the Man told him. "The creeps and punks are winning the fight. Sorry for the blunt talk, but that's the way I feel about it."

"Me, too, Mister President."

The Man had smiled. "Yeah, I know. You want to help wipe the puke off the Constitution and the flag of the United States?"

"Do I have a choice?"

"Sure. But hear me out first."

"Go ahead."

"If you don't want the job, you're suddenly discovered in a hospital where you've been in a coma for months. You're back to life."

"If I decide to do this . . . I'm a one-man wrecking crew?"

"Anywhere you can take an eighteen-wheeler."

"And I will be hauling real loads?"

"Most of the time."

He had lost everything. His wife, his business . . . he didn't even look like the same person. "I suppose the boys in the three-piece suits have a fancy code name all picked out for me?"

"Several have been suggested."

"Call me Dog."

"I like it. Any particular reason for that name?"

"I read a book once about a dog team. The government was supposed to have a kill team that was called the Dog Team."

"We did, before the liberals and the press decided they wanted to run the country."

Barry laughed aloud. This old boy had his finger on the problem all right. "I put the shots where I think they should go?"

"That's it in a nutshell. You'll be judge, jury, and executioner. But if you get out of control, you'll be dead within twenty-four hours. Do you understand that?"

"Perfectly clear. What happens when you leave office? This is your last term."

"Everything is set up. Doesn't make any difference who sits in the Oval Office. They can't stop you." He smiled. "They won't know anything about you."

"How does it work?"

"You really want to know, Dog?"

Barry gave that some thought. He finally concluded that the less he knew, the better off he'd be. "Forget I asked."

"Fine. After this meeting, we will never meet again. Your contact will be either Jackson or Weston. You remember them?"

Barry nodded.

The Man said, "I do not know you. I have never heard of you. I never want to hear from you."

"Fine with me."

"Anywhere there is trouble is where you'll go. You might be sent there. You might decide to go on your own. Most of the time, you'll make your own decisions."

"Good."

"I thought you'd like that."

"Weapons and high-tech backup equipment?"

"Anything the government has—short of nuclear weapons—can and will be provided for you. All you have to do is ask."

"I'm liking it more and more."

"You'll be contracted to the government. You'll be ramrodding an SST."

"I figured as much."

"You won't reconsider and have a partner?"

"I have a partner."

"Who?"

"My dog. Dog."

"Lone wolf all the way, huh?"

"I like it that way."

"You might be asked to give up your life. Do you fully understand that?"

"Yes. If that happens, I want Dog cared for."

"I'll make sure that all concerned understand that."

Barry and Dog walked out of the hospital and toward a midnight blue Kenworth parked across from the hospital grounds.

Barry made a visual inspection of the rig.

Midnight blue conventional with silver pinstriping. Smoked windows—legal. The best sound system on the market. Twin airhorns and twin remote-controlled spots. Forty-channel CB that with a switch could be boosted up enough to talk coast to coast . . . almost. Steer Safe stabilizers. Quartz halogen driving lights. Airglide 100 suspension. Alcoa aluminum 10-hole Budd wheels. Fuller Roadranger 13-speed transmission. The differentials were 3.73 Rockwells SQHP. Fontaine fifth wheel. Michelin steel-belt tires, 1100 by 24.5 tubeless. Air dryer for air brake. The mill was a 350 Cummins with Horton fan clutch. Jake brake. The sleeper was a VIP walk-in, robin's-egg-blue interior.

The bunk was Electro-warmth mattress with mirrors and 12-volt TV.

Dog ran around in circles, eager to be on the road once more.

And the memories came flooding almost painfully back to Barry. . . .

The dog sat by the Kenworth as if it had found a home. But he did not wag his tail at their approach.

"Oh, Barry!" Kate said. 'Look!" she pointed.

The animal was a husky, with perhaps some Siberian and malamute mixed in. The eyes were wolf-yellow, and mean looking

Kate knelt down and held out her hands. "Come on, boy," she urged.

The animal came to her, allowing the pretty lady to pet him.

"What's that on his collar?" Barry asked.

Kate loosened the wire that held the worn piece of paper. "A note." She read it aloud. "Goddamn dog bites. You find him, you keep him. He's two years old. Shots are due this fall. I named him Dog."

Barry tried very hard not to think about Kate. He was not very successful at it. He missed her terribly. And knew he always would, to one degree or another.

Barry helped the husky in and closed the door, settling down behind the wheel. He picked up the package lying on the floorboards.

He hesitated only briefly before opening it. His new life was contained within the thick package. It was a beginning.

He carefully opened the packet. New York State driver's license. Barry Rivera. He had been told it was a real address. He had never been there.

The Kenworth was his home. From now on. Forever.

Until he died—or was killed. There was no retirement plan for Barry Rivera or Dog.

And not much of a choice for either man or animal.

He checked the credit cards. Dozens of them. Cards for stores he'd never heard of. Chains in every state of the Union. He would never want for anything. The bills would be spread out over dozens of federal agencies. If he needed cash, he could use one of the many bank cards available. No credit limit on any card.

Barry looked older than his years. Sometime during his coma, gray had crept into his hair, which was salt and pepper now. The operations had changed his looks forever. Even Dog had changed. He was no longer the playful animal Kate had found in that truck stop parking lot. Dog looked savage, and could be just that.

"Going to be interesting, Dog."

Dog growled, rumbling deep in his throat.

Sitting in the Kenworth, Barry looked at Dog. Dog spoke to him in that funny-odd husky way. Doggy talk, Kate had called it.

Barry pushed Kate from his mind. "You ready to roll, Dog?"

Dog was ready.

Whoever had placed the packet in the cab had cranked the big diesel, warming it up for Barry. Barry checked his gauges and slipped the rig into gear.

Dog and Dog pulled out.

Two

He had been on the road for two months. No action yet. He had driven to Louisiana and seen his brother. His brother was a ranting, raving loony . . . and would be that way until the day he died. Barry had iced his ex-partner and for weeks had been working the roads in his SST. Safe Secure Transport. His first destination had been St. Louis. But he was paged in a truck stop and found out it was just a normal routine run, carrying some mysterious government cargo.

Now he was sitting in a truck stop just outside St. Louis, drinking coffee and listening to the other drivers talk.

He listened to them talk about what coops were open and which ones were closed. Listened to them jaw about the new 65-mph speed limit, and how they could pick up another hundred miles a day with it . . . maybe then they'd break even.

Barry felt eyes on him and lifted his own, meeting the gaze of the man across the U-shaped counter.

"Howdy," the man said.

Had to come sooner or later, Barry. Running into someone he'd known, back in his other life. Barry nodded his head in acknowledgment.

"I seen you pull in. That's a damn nice rig."

"If you're gonna go broke, might as well do it first class," Barry said with a smile.

"Ain't that the truth! I didn't mean to stare. It's just that you remind me of a fellow I used to know."

And I know you, too, Beer-Butt. "Oh?"

"Yeah. Fellow name of Barry Rivers."

"Didn't I read something about him; hear it on the TV? Something about his truck blew up or something like that. Some time back."

"Yeah. Up in Virginia. His wife's name was Kate. Sweetest little girl you ever did see."

"Shut your damn mouth about Kate!" another trucker said. "I knew her, too. Poor little thing. Let the dead lie." He shook his head and grimaced, then smiled at Beer-Butt. "Sorry, Buddy. Forget it. Kate was special to a lot of us."

But more to me, Barry thought. *So much, much more to me.*

Kate had been loved and cherished by truckers from coast to coast, border to border. But touch her, brother, and either you were stomped to death by other drivers, or you wished you were dead.

The driver who had spoken sharply tossed some money on the counter, picked up his check, and walked away.

Beer-Butt was again looking at him. "You got a name?"

"Rivera."

Beer-Butt cocked his head from side to side, studying Barry. "Rivera. What's your handle? Mine's Beer-Butt." He laughed and patted his big belly. As good-humored as ever.

Barry's mind was racing. No point in lying about it. When he spoke, it was very soft. "Dog."

Beer-Butt spilled hot coffee all over his big hands. The waitress came over, mopped up the mess, poured Beer-Butt another cup, and told him this time, try to hit his mouth. Beer-Butt picked up the cup and moved around the counter, sitting down beside Barry, staring at him closely. His big, broad face was pale under his tan.

"It's eerie, man. You even look sorta like him." He shook his head. "But . . . no. I went to his and Kate's funeral."

"What are you talking about?"

"Even the voice is the same. Mister, where you been runnin' the last couple of years?"

"Alaska. Pay's good, but I got tired of that shit."

"I heard that. But you do look like Big Joe's son."

"This fellow who got killed—he must have been quite a guy."

"Oh, yeah, man. He sure as hell was that, and more."

Felt very odd, having someone discuss you in the past tense.

"Big Joe never really got over it. He died two months ago."

That shook Barry right down to his cowboy boots. Somebody should have told him. Goddammit, they should have told him.

When he could once more trust himself to speak, Barry said, "This Big Joe, he owned a trucking company?"

"Rivers Trucking. We still carry it under his name. Probably always will. All us truckers went together and bought it. It was odd . . . lawyers said there was no way the government was gonna loan us that money. But you know, that loan application was approved and back in *one week!* You ever heard of such a thing in all your born days?"

It always helps to have somebody in your corner, Barry thought. *Like the President of the United States, the Treasury, and the FBI.* "That's odd, all right. No other family around, huh?"

"Huh? Oh, Rivers, you mean. Yeah . . . a daughter over in Texas. But she didn't want any part of it. We bought it from her."

At least he had some family left. "This Kate y'all were speaking of . . . she must have been really something."

Beer-Butt smiled gently. "That she was, my boy. An angel with a gutter mouth. Man, she could cuss!"

Barry remembered that vividly. Then he made a great show of checking his watch. "Well, I got to roll."

"Yeah, me, too. Headin' to the house."

"Where's home?"

"New Orleans. Where's your home?"

"That rig out yonder in the lot."

"I know the feelin'. Hey, you know what? You oughta get you a dog. They're good company."

Barry smiled. "I might just do that." He picked up his check. "See you around."

There was a man waiting in the shadows by Barry's rig. Barry slowed his step. But Dog was not barking or growling. And Dog was not friendly toward strangers.

"You stay in the shadows, and I'll do the same," the man spoke, just audibly over the rumble of many diesels.

"All right."

"That was a close one in there, with Beer-Butt."

"Yeah, but it's all right."

"It's never all right. He's the type who'll think on it hard. Then he'll confide in some of his coworkers. But that's not too bad. Not the way I see it; not the way Weston sees it. . . ."

This then was Jackson. Barry finally made him out.

"We've discussed the possibilities of this happening."

"And?"

"They'd help you. They owe us. Uncle Sam giveth, Uncle Sam can taketh away."

"Their trucking company?"

"You got it."

"I don't think you'd have to go that far with those guys."

"Neither do I. Damn, but they're a randy bunch."

"Why in the fuck didn't you tell me my old man was dead?"

"Because we didn't want you screwing up and trying to attend the funeral. Think about it, and you'll see the reasoning."

He thought about it. Jackson was right. Barry had worked for the Agency; he knew how cold it had to be at times. "All right."

Jackson patted the fender of the Kenworth. "Always wanted to drive one of these. Never did learn how."

"Stick to super-spooking, Jackson. It pays more, and it's a hell of a lot safer, believe me."

Jackson laughed softly. "For some strange reason, I believe you."

"You're not here to engage in idle chitchat. What's on your mind?"

Jackson laid a newspaper on the fender of the Kenworth. "Dane County is a cesspool. See what you think about it."

Then he walked off into the darkness, vanishing amid the mass of parked rigs.

Barry picked up the newspaper and unlocked his door. He let Dog out to do his business and waited until the animal returned. He climbed into the tractor, made sure the doors were secure, and stepped into his sleeper, stretching out and clicking on the bedlamp.

It didn't take him long to agree with Jackson. Dane County was, indeed, a reeking cesspool. Jackson had written: *Maybe someone ought to drain it?*

He rolled across southern Illinois and stayed with Interstate 64 through Louisville and Lexington before angling off. Just after leaving the interstate, he pulled off into a truck stop. He let Dog out, keeping an eye on the animal so he wouldn't lap up any spilled antifreeze from overheated engines. Ethylene glycol was toxic, and there was usually plenty of it around fuel stops. For some strange reason, dogs like the taste of it.

He ordered lunch at the counter and ate while listening to other drivers jaw about this and that. Then he heard what he had hoped to hear.

"Anybody here goin' into Dane County?"

The U-shaped counter filled with truckers became unusually silent. One trucker finally broke the silence. "I ain't lost a damn thing in Dane County, man."

The other truckers chuckled, but it was subdued laughter. Strained. The driver who had asked the question looked around. "I'm new here, boys. Just tryin' to test the waters. What's the matter with Dane County?"

The waitress handling that portion of the station, a woman who looked to be in her mid-fifties, spoke up. "The Anson family is what's wrong with it."

Barry looked up. "I been haulin' in Canada and Alaska for the past two years. Got tired of the cold. I heard that Anson Trucking was hirin'. I'd hate to know I run all this way for nothing."

A trucker said, "Oh, they're always hirin', buddy, but take a tip from an old hand. Stay out of Dane County." He picked up his check and left.

Barry looked at the driver who'd first asked about Dane County. "What do you think?"

"I got to work. Payments on that Peterbilt don't stop."

"What are you drivin'?"

"379."

The men shook hands. Toby Kendall. Barry said, "I'm like you. I got to work." He looked at the waitress. "You wanna open up just a little bit more on Dane County?"

She eyeballed them suspiciously. "How do I know you boys don't work for the Ansons; sent in here to spy and snoop?"

"I guess you don't, ma'am," Toby said. He was, Barry guessed, in his early thirties. An open, honest face. "My home's in Alabama."

"My rig is my home," Barry said, "but I carry a New York State driver's license."

She looked around. The place was quiet; no one at her station. She began wiping the counter, talking as she worked. "Dane County is owned by the Anson family. Lock, stock, and barrel. There are three towns in the county. All owned by the Anson family. One sheriff, three chiefs of police. All of them in the pocket of Maxwell Anson. The whole Anson family, kids and all, is nothin' but rich white trash. The kids get in trouble, Maxwell buys them out of it. The sheriff, Jud Manville, is owned by the Ansons. That tell you boys anything at all?"

"How's he treat his drivers?" Toby asked.

"All right, as long as you don't object to what you're draggin' around behind you on the road."

"I . . . I don't understand," Barry questioned.

She stared at him. "Why don't you boys go to work for J.B. Hunt? Forget about Dane County. I ain't sayin' no more." She walked away.

"Where'd you hear about Anson Truckin'?" Toby asked.

"St. Louis. At a rest stop. I just thought I'd check it out, that's all."

"You still game?"

"Hell, why not?"

Two women, mother and daughter, Cathy and April Monroe, had been found in their New York State registered BMW just inside the Tennessee line. They had been horribly raped and sexually abused . . . in every manner possible. "Disgusting" was the word the reporter had chosen to describe their treatment. When Cathy's husband, father of April, had flown down from New York to positively identify the bodies, he had received a tip that the women had been raped and murdered in Dane County, Kentucky. Mr. Monroe had gone up to Dane County. He had never returned. He was presumed dead. His body had never been found.

That had been a couple of months back. The police had dropped their investigation.

Barry had elected not to tell Toby what he knew about Dane County . . . which was damn little.

Barry was going into whatever faced him almost blind.

Toby followed Barry toward Dane County. "You got a handle?" he radioed.

"Dog."

"Lucky."

We'll probably need it, Barry thought.

They rolled into Dane County, past factories that carried the Anson name, past exits to coal mines that belonged to Anson. No question about it—the county belonged to Maxwell Anson.

They parked their rigs in the lot of a nice motel—the Anson Inn, naturally.

Barry was not really surprised to find a sealed envelope waiting for him at the desk. If Toby took notice of it, he did not let on.

"Your rooms are right around the corner, gentlemen," the young woman said. "Last two on your left. Twenty-eight and Thirty. It'll be peaceful at night."

"Our rigs OK where they are?" Toby asked.

"Just fine."

Barry laid a credit card on the counter. "Both the rooms," he instructed the woman. Toby started to protest, but Barry waved him silent. "Pay me later. I been workin' steady in the deep freeze, makin' good money."

"The deep freeze?" the desk clerk questioned.

"Alaska." Barry smiled at her and she returned the smile.

A very pretty woman, almost beautiful. One of those blondes the Southern part of the nation grew so well. A healthy, glowing-with-life shock of honey-blond hair tumbling about a heart-shaped face. Flawless complexion. Full lips, violet eyes that would probably darken during the sex act. About five-five with a figure that was guaran-damn-teed to turn heads.

She made Barry painfully aware that he had not known a woman, sexually, in a long time.

Something about this woman—Barry guessed her age at about twenty-five—drew him to her. . . .

He shook that off as best he could. There was no room in his life for any serious attachments.

When he again met her eyes, he saw interest in the violet. He smiled; she returned the smile. He dropped his eyes to her name tag pinned just above her left breast. Brenda.

She followed his eyes. "Hooks. Brenda Hooks, Mister Rivera."

"Very pleased to meet you, Brenda. Would you recommend the food here at the inn?"

"I sure would," a man said. Barry turned. Toby had already gone to his room. A man, his wife, and two teenage girls were walking out of the dining area. The man smiled and nodded. The girls smiled. Very pretty dark-haired girls.

"Sol Wiseman," Brenda said. "Real nice man and lovely kids. His wife is very nice. Yes, I would recommend the food here. That is, if you're looking for homestyle cooking and not something city-fancy."

"Home style sound great."

"Enjoy your stay, Mister Rivera."

"Thank you."

In his room—and it was a surprisingly nice room—Barry took off his boots and opened the thick envelope and began to read.

The Anson family did indeed own it all. Maxwell Anson was the leader of the clan. Fifty-five years old and a widower. Had six kids. Five sons and one daughter. Barry laughed when he read the sons' nicknames: Banger, Slapper, Whacker, Eddie, and Bugger. He was surprised he didn't find a hambone or a woollyhumper in among them.

"Where in the hell do they get these names?" he muttered.

And how, he pondered, do I prowl in country on my off-time? Then he remembered the camera. A top-of-the-line 35mm with all the accessories.

So I'll take pictures as a hobby. That's a good way to prowl.

He went back to the dossier.

Daughter's name was Jennifer. A real looker, but haughty and arrogant, and with an evil, mean streak in her. Her best friend was one Jane Causy. Pretty. Ralph Causy was the second in command of the Anson empire. Like Jennifer Anson, Jane screwed like a rabbit.

Bugger, Slapper, Whacker, Eddie, and Banger were pure scum. Rich scum, but still scum. White trash. Had been in trouble since the day they popped out of the womb. Bully boys, local terrorists—hillbilly style. Brutal.

A lot a good, fine, very decent people in Dane County. But any number of real nasties as well.

And for all the trouble the boys had been in, none of them had ever served a day behind bars. And had never served any military time, either. Banger and Slapper should have, but their number was never called back during the draft. Daddy's money again.

Anson was named after great-great-granddad Anson. They were all crooks, the whole damn family tree crawled with evil. Sickening reading.

Barry laid it aside. He'd get back to it.

But the next paragraph caught and held his attention. He picked up the dossier.

The whole county was about to break loose; the good people had had a bellyful of it.

Things should be getting interesting in Dane County, Kentucky.

Three

Dog walked Dog, but the dossier kept pulling at him. Finally he gave up and returned to his room, once more picking up the dossier, and studied the attached photographs.

The Anson sons were anything but handsome, with pus-guts and piggy, narrow eyes, cruel slits for mouths. But surprisingly enough, the young lady of the Anson clan was near beautiful . . . but pouty. And with the same cruel look about her.

What had the waitress said . . . rich white trash.

She had known what she was talking about.

The great great-grandfather had begun his fortune as a horse thief and slave trader. His son had gone one step further and had become a whoremonger . . . among other things. He had been a perverted man—as, Barry suspected, were the present-day group—much into beatings and torture of a strange sexual nature.

Grandfather Anson had amassed a rather large fortune, operating unsafe coal mines and paying his miners the minimum. John L. Lewis and friends had never made a dent in Dane County. Grandfather Anson had the company store and paid many of his workers scrip . . . redeemable only at an Anson store. Virtual white slavery. A lot of men—no one knew how many for certain because of the deliberately faulty record keeping—had died in Anson mines. One historian had put the number at over five hundred.

A horrible but almost tangible impression came to Barry: of airless shafts deep in the ground; of men screaming and choking and gasping for breath; of poisonous gas and rotting, unsafe timbers; of cave-ins and explosions; of long-dead and mute skeletons.

Barry shook his head. "Nice people."

The present patriarch of the Anson Clan, Maxwell, was a bit more subtle in his business dealings, but was still considered a crook . . . simply a more educated one.

His sons, however, were a different breed of polecat.

They had, to a man, failed in school, none of them even graduating from high school. Their intelligence was above average; they just didn't care.

The more Barry read, the more it appeared to him that none of the Anson clan was worth the gunpowder it would take to blow their brains out.

Banger and Slapper were the county's most widely known bullies. All the boys were big men, six feet or better, two hundred plus pounds. And pus-gutted. Still very strong, but going to lard. They were feared brawlers, and would use any weapon if the fight was not going their way.

"Bear that in mind," Barry noted.

All the boys—Banger, Slapper, Whacker, Eddie, and Bugger—were notorious womanizers, who either got their way with women—or else they would just take what they wanted.

Real nice fellows.

The next paragraph, no matter how many times

Barry read it, always filled him with a curious mixture of rage and pity: rage toward the Anson clan, pity for the victims of their perversion. The game began with getting the victim into their power. All the Anson boys had been known to keep, and were still keeping, certain poor families—both black and white—deep in debt—to the Anson boys of course. Five-for-ten loans with no chance of ever catching up. When the breadwinner of the family, usually the father, finally realized it was hopeless, that he would be in debt for the rest of his life (or go to prison, for it was all done with semilegal paper), one of the Anson boys would suggest an alternative to being stomped into the ground or jailed.

The man would have little choice but to stand by and watch helplessly as the pick of his daughters was herded out and paraded like a cow in an auction barn.

After a reasonable length of time—the period set by whatever brother—a portion of the debt would be erased. But never all of it.

Slapper was famous for winking to his buddies, a ragtag assortment of rednecks and hoods, and saying, "I ain't never in the shorts when it comes to pussy, boys."

Barry rubbed his eyes, thinking, *Somebody in Justice or Treasury or the Bureau spent some time in here putting all this together, and somebody very high up, like in Sugar Cube, doesn't want this to go through the ridiculous farce known as our judicial system.*

"Suits the shit out of me," Barry spoke to Dog. Dog agreed.

Banger was particularly offensive with his less than subtle blackmailing. Since Banger was supposedly hung like the proverbial bull, he liked to take the unfortunate man's wife—if she was pretty enough—and have sex with her—while the husband watched. Usually, after being beaten and stomped into submission by the other brothers and their punky friends, he could do little about it. Not with the threat of Anson millions hanging over his head; not with the threat of one of his girls being raped in front of his eyes. And his land would usually have a mortgage on it, held by the Bank of Anson. Owned by Ansons.

Barry found it sickening. He wondered how long it had been going on. And why hadn't someone done something to stop it?

But he knew why. The mayor would be in Anson's pocket. The county DA would be snuggled in there with him. The sheriff. The chief of police. The city commission. Anybody who was somebody would have reached that plateau of success because of Anson help. They would owe it all to the Anson family.

And many of Dane County's less fortunate citizens, the victims, would be of pioneer stock, distrustful of authorities, too proud to ask for help, fearful of the law, especially the "High Sheriff." They would always nurture the hope, however slim, that some day, some way, they would work their way out of the hole that had been dug for them . . . with their own help. But they never seemed to find a big enough shovel.

Maybe this time, Barry thought, the shovel was on the way. Or was already here.

All the sons were married except for Bugger. Bugger liked young girls. Twelve or thirteen. All the married sons had children; all were said to physically abuse their wives and kids.

He closed the file and tucked it away in the bottom of his shaving kit.

Barry was not known as a terribly compassionate man, was not filled with overflowing sympathy for many of the nation's so-called downtrodden. He had great love and compassion for the very young and the elderly and the physically handicapped. Very little for anyone in between those limits. He believed that most people could help themselves if only they would. Many, he felt, simply would not. They would not take advantage of educational facilities offered them. They would not break away from home boundaries to better themselves. Their position was always, "somebody else's fault." Being from the South, Barry knew only too well that the class system was very much alive and well in all parts of the nation. Always had been, always would be.

On a scale of one to ten, Barry would give Anson, Kentucky, about a three on beauty. Maybe a two. The town was singularly unspectacular. The valley in which it sat was beautiful. He walked the town's main section, mentally setting in his mind the lay of the small town.

Miller's Hardware, Smith's Drugstore, Wiseman's Department Store, the Beanery—Good Eats.

The courthouse sat in the middle of the square, the main shopping area surrounding the old building on all four sides. Some obscure Civil War colonel stood immortalized, carved in stone, frozen in time as he waved his saber, urging his troops onward and forward to victory, his gallant mount reared up on his hind legs. Man and beast were covered with bird shit.

Barry looked at the name. Colonel Anson. Figured.

He walked on. He waited for the light to change and stepped out onto the street, jumping back just in time to avoid being hit by a speeding pickup truck, whose driver paid no attention to traffic lights. What a pickup—a redneck's dream. At least six antennas on it, twin spotlights, fog lights, chrome roll bars, twin pipes running up the sides of the cab—chrome, of course—mud flaps front and rear, big rearing stallion for a hood ornament, Rebel flag in the rear window, and every other accessory that could be placed on a vehicle.

It looked like a child gone wild in a toy store.

A child monster, for Barry had seen the face of the man driving the truck, before it went speeding up the main street. Banger Anson.

He had walked a block back toward the motel when a cop car slid beside him, pulling in to the curb. Barry waited as the deputy got out and walked up to him. He was not an unfriendly type; that could be read on his face.

"Howdy," the deputy said.

"Deputy, I do something wrong?"

"Naw. I seen you almost gettin' run over by that pickup. Can I see some I.D., please?"

Barry handed him his driver's license. "The lunatic driving that truck ran a red light. He should be ticketed."

The deputy smiled. "I didn't see that, but it don't surprise me. That's Banger Anson."

"Is that supposed to impress me?"

The deputy shrugged. "It impresses a whole bunch of folks around these parts." He handed Barry's license to him.

"Are you one of them?"

"I just do my job, Mister Rivera. And that includes checkin' out new people who come to town."

"Well, I came here to apply for a job with Anson Trucking. But if Banger is representative of the Anson family, I think I'll just take a short vacation and to hell with Anson Trucking."

"You shore don't talk like no truck driver."

"The man driving that truck is a menace on the streets and highways."

The deputy chose to ignore that. "I'll give you a personal-like warnin', Mister Rivera: you watch your mouth about the Anson family around here. They rule the roost in this henhouse."

"They peck on everyone, but no one pecks on them, right?"

"You may be from the city, but you know somethin' about a henhouse. Off the record . . . yeah, that's shore enough one way of puttin' it."

Barry got a strong impression the deputy was not the uneducated hillbilly he was pretending very hard to portray. But if so, he mused, why the act?

"I've been around a few farms, yes."

"Uh-huh. Tell me, Mister Rivera, are you plannin' on stayin' long in Dane County?"

"Well, it certainly seems like an interesting county."

"That ain't exactly what I asked, but I guess it'll have to do."

"Photography is a hobby of mine. I might prowl around and take some shots."

"With a camera, I hope," the deputy drawled.

The deputy's smile held a bit more than humor.

That, deputy, was the worst accent I have ever heard. You might be fooling these people around here, but not me. The man was not who he claimed to be. Not entirely. The accent just was not right. It was forced, as if it had deliberately been educated out of the man, and he was attempting to regain it.

"Where can a man get a drink around this place, Deputy?"

"Drinkin' is agin the law in this county, Mister Rivera."

Barry cringed at the accent. "Well, I'm really not that much of a drinker."

"Is 'at raight?"

Jesus Christ! Barry thought. *Deputy, you are a fraud.*

" 'At's what a lot of folks 'round here say, but they's a heap of 'em manage to get drunk a lot." The deputy's name tag read: G. Kildare.

"I understand," Barry said.

Something clouded the lawman's eyes. "Maybe you do, maybe you don't. Well, you be careful now, Mister Rivera, you hear? And do en-joy your visit with us." He walked off to his car, his boots clopping on the sidewalk.

After the deputy had left, Barry looked around him. Without staring at them, he noticed a big-bellied, broad-shouldered man standing with two other men by the pickup that had almost struck him. It was obvious the men were related. They all looked like hogs. They stood watching him walk away.

Banger, Slapper, and Whacker Anson.

Something dark and primal reared up silently within Barry. He struggled to control the urge to kill. *Don't step out of character yet,* he cautioned himself. *Just play it cool.*

He walked back to the motel. Brenda was alone, behind the desk. He stepped inside and chatted with her, telling her of his hobby.

"An amateur photographer. That's interesting, Mister Rivera."

"Barry. Yes, this seems to be an interesting county. I'll just roam around a bit."

"Oh, it's a very interesting place, Mis . . . Barry. Just be sure you have permission."

That set him back a bit. "Permission? Permission to drive public roads?"

"This is Dane County, Barry. Anson country. Believe me when I say the Anson family does not take kindly to outsiders coming in and snooping around."

Barry chuckled. "I'm not a writer, Brenda. I just like to take pictures of things that interest me. Old homes, lovely meadows and fields . . . things of that nature. I'm not looking for any skeletons to rattle."

He noticed Brenda's eyes shift and widen, fright touching them. Then the voice spoke from behind him.

"Takin' pictures of purty meadows and sich. Ain't 'at sweet? What are you, anyways, some kind of goddamn queer?"

Four

Barry turned slowly. Bugger Anson. All six feet two inches and two hundred and thirty pounds of pus-gut and mouth and sick perversion. In the flash of a second, time spun Barry back to his childhood when he'd been recovering from a bout of fever that had laid him flat on his back for months, and how he had suffered at the hands of that type of person he hated most of all . . . the bully.

"Sissy boy, sissy boy!" they had taunted him. For a time. Unable to participate in anything physical while recovering, Barry had been forced to endure the taunting.

He had walked on, doing his best to ignore them. Some of them had enjoyed running up to him, slamming into him, knocking him sprawling, sometimes bloodying his knees and elbows.

But they hadn't been able to make him cry.

An elderly black gentleman had watched the painful taunting for several weeks, sitting on the front porch of his house in New Orleans, watching through sad eyes. After one particularly painful session, he had called Barry to the porch, sat him down, and dabbed iodine on the cuts.

"You don't cry, boy," the man had said. "Why is that?"

"I won't give them the satisfaction," Barry had replied. "But I will have mine, someday."

"And just how do you propose to do that? They're all much bigger and stronger than you."

"Probably with a club."

The man smiled. "Just be careful that you don't kill one of them."

Barry had looked puzzled. "Why not? Would that be some sort of great loss?"

The old man had looked closely at the boy who spoke adult words. He did not know how to reply. If he answered it truthfully, that no, it would be no loss to the world—nits grew into lice—the boy just might pick up a tire iron and smash in the head of one of his tormentors . . . which was what they deserved.

So the man had said nothing.

"I tell my dad I hurt myself playing."

"Does he believe you?"

"I don't know."

The black man had smiled. "I think you'll make it, son."

"Oh, I'll make it."

The next week, Barry had stepped out from an alley and smacked a bully in the face with a 2 x 4, fracturing the punk's skull.

It had taken only two more ambushes from the club-wielding young boy for the other young savages to learn they had best leave him alone. . . .

Barry met Bugger's gaze. "No, I like the ladies. Which way do you lean?"

"Whut you mean by 'at, boy?" Bugger felt he just might have been insulted, but he wasn't real sure.

Barry stared at him.

Bugger was a veteran brawler, smart enough to read

a man's eyes. Knew how to detect calmness, confidence, and the ability to win. And this dude standing in the lobby of Miss Brenda's place was no pansy. Bugger took in the thick wrists, the lean waist, the heavy arms, and the flat-knuckled hands.

Bugger didn't know what to do; didn't want to lose no face in front of Miss Brenda, 'cause he had dreams—some of them quite vivid—of jerking down Miss Brenda's panties and seeing if that honey-blond hair extended all the way down.

Suddenly Barry smiled and extended his hand to Bugger. Bugger stared at it. "Barry Rivera. Nice to meet you, Mister . . . ?"

Bugger grabbed the hand and shook it before he thought. He released it quickly. "Bugger!"

"Bugger. How quaint. It fits you."

"Ah . . . thanks."

"You're quite welcome. Perhaps we'll meet another day." Barry turned his back to the man. He could not help but notice Brenda quickly lowering her head, hiding her smile. He had made points with her.

Bugger mumbled something under his breath and walked out of the lobby. The door closed behind him.

"He comes in every day to stand and stare at me," Brenda said. "He is probably the most repulsive person I have ever encountered." She smiled. "But I could have gotten rich selling tickets to that performance."

"Oh?"

She laughed, a good hearty laugh. "Bugger Anson, Barry."

"He didn't impress me; his type never has. How did he pick up his nickname?"

She blushed. "I . . . ah . . . don't know you well enough to answer that."

"Then how do I get to know you well enough?"

"Time, Barry." She turned away, then looked back at him. "That rig you're driving probably cost over a hundred thousand dollars. And you neither look like nor act like nor talk like a down-at-the-heels truck driver. Mister Barry Rivera, you better be who you say you are. Sheriff Manville will check you out; be certain of that. You just made Bugger Anson look like the fool he is, and one of my cleaning ladies heard it all. The story will get around town, believe me."

"Why are you warning me?"

"Maybe to keep you from getting hurt." Her eyes flicked over his heavily muscled arms and shoulders. "Although that might take some doing. Service time, Barry?"

"Special Forces. Captain, A-Team."

"You've led an interesting life."

"Yes." *More than you will ever know, unfortunately.* "It's been nice talking with you, Brenda. Perhaps we'll see each other again." *Soon, I hope.*

"I'm sure we will." She smiled. Her teeth were very white and perfectly formed.

He settled in. He made up his mind to forget about applying for a job with Anson Trucking. He had a hunch if he stuck around, they'd come to him . . . one way or the other. He wasn't worried about any checking the sheriff might do. He would stand up under it.

There was no law against a man taking a vacation. And he had a hefty bank account that was real. The law couldn't arrest him for vagrancy. Hell, the truck alone would stop that.

He had a light dinner, and reread the dossier on the Ansons. He hoped it would not give him nightmares.

Barry slept well and deeply; no one disturbed his sleep. If Dog had growled during the night, he had not even heard him.

As he was eating a good country breakfast in the Anson Inn dining room—ham and eggs, grits and home fries, juice, coffee, and biscuits—he made a point of asking his waitress where in the county he could find some old homes, in ruins or getting that way. He would like to photograph them. His hobby. She told him, naming half a dozen. She specifically mentioned the Blasingame ruins.

One man in the dining room seemed to be making an all-out effort not to look at Barry, but at the same time to listen to what was being said. Barry recognized him as the second man in the pickup truck the day before.

He rose from the table, leaving a tip and smiling at the waitress. "I think I'll travel out to that Blasingame house you told me about. I probably won't get lost more than a dozen times."

She returned the smile. One of the nice people in the county, Barry thought; and there were certainly many more nice ones than those aligned with the Anson family.

"You be careful, now, you hear?" she cautioned him. "And if you get lost, you just get on the CB and start hollerin'. Somebody will be along directly."

Barry thanked her for her concern and walked out of the dining room, up to the front desk. "OK if I drop my trailer where it is, Brenda?"

"Sure. It's out of the way. Oh, Toby pulled out this morning. Said to thank you, but he didn't like the smell in Dane County."

"I wonder what happened."

"I think he had a run-in with one of the Anson boys."

"Too bad; seemed like a nice fellow. Well, I'll be gone for the rest of the day, Brenda. Taking pictures."

She nodded, and without looking up, said, "That lean, hawk-faced man in there is Banger's right-hand man. Lewis Kern. He and his brothers, Dave, Hammer, and Freddie, all work for the Anson clan. And they are all mean. They're some of the enforcers. If you know what I mean."

He nodded.

"The bottom line is that he was asking questions about you this morning."

"What did you tell him?"

"That your comings and goings were your business and absolutely no concern of mine . . . or of his."

Barry chuckled. "You don't like the Ansons very much, do you, Brenda?"

"No." She met his eyes, the violet now serious. "And neither do you, Mister Barry Rivera. Or whatever your name is."

"It's Rivera. What time do you get off, Brenda?"

She blinked. "Why—five o'clock."

"And where do you live?"

She smiled. "One two five Elm."

"And where might that be?"

"You're standing in it."

"You live here? At the inn?"

"Right directly across the court from you. I am owner/manager of this motel."

"Well, I am impressed. Would it be terribly forward and presumptuous of me to ask you out to dinner this evening?"

"Why, heavens, suh!" She mimed old Southern. "Ah have just met you!"

"Please forgive my lack of courtly graces. You see, I'm a damn Yankee. Will you have dinner with me?"

"I will meet you in yonder," she drawled, jerking a thumb toward the dining room. "At seven. Sharp."

"As you wish, ma'am."

"Suh," she said, smiling.

Walking back to his room, Barry felt better than he had in months.

His Kenworth had been reworked by government people while he was in the hospital. It would take an expert to find the hidden compartments containing his weapons. He carried two M-10's, with barrel extension/silencer. Case of ammo for both. He had a case of mixed grenades, HE and WP. Colt Woodsman with silencer. Extra clips for all. Ammo. Browning 9mm, clips, leather. He had a ten-pound chunk of C-4, timers, dets . . . and a few other items stashed in the floor of his trailer.

He dropped his trailer and tucked the Colt behind his belt, his shirt hanging over the butt. He drove off in the general direction of the Blasingame ruins.

Checking his mirrors from time to time, he saw he was not being followed. He turned on his CB and scanner. The red light darted helter-skelter back and forth, catching only bits of conversation. Then it stopped.

". . . headin' out toward the Blasingame place."

"Ain't but one way to git out there and back that he'd take. Les'n he wanted to git los'. So you jist sit there at the junction and wait it out."

"Aw, Slapper. I—"

"Do as yore tol', boy!"

"Yessir."

Barry drove on, toward the ruins. They were a sad yet magnificent sight, a fading reminder of the pomp and glory of what had been. Standing in front of the huge columns—just about all that was left of the mansion except for a few crumbling walls—Barry felt his deep South heritage tug at him; the roots were buried deep.

He shot the ruins from as many angles as possible. He had always had a gift for photography, and he wanted these to be right. He wished to God he'd brought a light meter. He knew that he had several truly exceptional shots of the place, with the huge oaks in the background; another shot was from inside the ruins, silhouetting the great columns against the sky.

He almost lost himself in his work, almost forgetting who he was and what he had now become. Almost.

But that was something he could never afford to forget.

He drove around the country, very much aware that after a time, he had picked up a tail. And they were not very good at it.

He stopped for lunch at a little country store, dining on crackers and cheese and a Coke. Then he continued his roaming.

Back at the motel, his trained eyes picked up quickly that his room had been tossed, and not by experts either. They had made some effort to conceal their clumsy endeavors, but to Barry, the search stood out like that much-talked-about sore thumb.

He wondered, as he showered, shaved, and dressed for dinner, if he had passed inspection. He felt he had. But he knew that the longer he stayed, the more he would be watched . . . and the more careful he would have to be.

He was directed to a small, private dining room in the rear of the main dining area of the inn. He spoke to the Wiseman family, thinking that they really must like the food, then stepped into the private part of the area. One look at Brenda and he smiled with pleasure.

She was lovely.

She was wearing a dress. Barry knew little of women's fashions; could not tell whether the garment was currently in vogue or not. But Brenda filled it out in all the right places, and the V-neckline showed just enough cleavage to make him realize what he'd like to have for dessert. Her long hair framed her lovely face, and she wore a simple gold chain around her neck.

"Brenda, have you been waiting long?"

"About a minute. You look very nice in a suit."

"You're beautiful," he said and meant it.

She smiled up at him, waiting until he was seated, then asked, "How did your work go today?"

"Very well, thank you. That old place was magnificent. But sadly so."

She cocked her head, the gesture almost heartbreakingly lovely. "Well, maybe you *are* what you say you are."

He smiled mysteriously, knowing with an inbred insight that this woman could be trusted. "And maybe not."

"Yes. That is probably closer to the truth. But if you're playing a game, Barry, it's a very dangerous one."

"So is truck driving, my dear."

She laughed and picked up her menu. They talked low and long—before, during, and after dinner. Each seemed to be captivated by the other. It had been a lovely dinner, but neither of them could, if asked, have told what they had just eaten without effort. They had been too busy staring at each other.

After dinner, they went walking.

". . . three years at the university," Brenda was saying, "then it was going to be the Peace Corps. Save the world and all that." She paused.

They had checked on Dog, and then they had changed; Brenda into jeans and a T-shirt, Barry into jeans, boots, and a western shirt. They had left Dog sleeping peacefully in the room.

It was nice walking, hands, shoulders, and occasionally hips brushing. Barry had forgotten how nice taking a walk with a lovely woman could be. "And then?" he prompted.

She looked up at him, her eyes shining in the faint light from a street lamp. She sighed, hesitated, and then seemed to make up her mind about this rugged-looking man that had just stepped, or driven, into her life.

A city cop unit drove by, a man seated behind the cage in the back seat.

"I feel sorry for him," Brenda said. "They enjoy beating prisoners at the jail."

"Haven't any of these people in Dane County learned about constitutional rights and reporting things to the feds?" There was a note of exasperation in the question.

"You don't understand, Barry. These are mountain folks. They do things differently."

"If you say so. What were you about to say?"

She sighed. "OK. Barry, I feel—well, safe with you. Silly thing to say; I don't even know you. Except"—she looked up at him—"that there is much more to you than you're telling. But I've got to trust somebody. And you seem to have entered my life at the right time—I hope it's right. If I'm wrong about you, I'll sure learn my lesson the hard way. And that, buddy, is a double play on words." She said the last bitterly.

Barry knew what she meant.

The Anson boys would have a high ol' time passing Miss Brenda around during a gang-bang. And they would do it . . . if they got the chance.

But he meant to see that that chance would never come.

"I won't even attempt to unravel all that spiel, Brenda. But I'll admit that I'm intrigued by the statement that you have to trust someone. Also that bit about learning a lesson. Care to explain?"

"I think you know. I think you know all about the Anson boys and how they treat women."

"How would I know?"

"Because I think you work for the government. And, oh, Barry, if you do . . . be careful."

He did not reply.

She blinked several times; studied his face in silence. "Let's go take a ride in your truck. I like big trucks. I guess I do. I've never ridden in one."

Looking down at her, lips shining in the glow of the night's overhanging chandelier of astral worlds whose single flash of brilliance now seemed solely at and for them, Barry wanted very badly to taste those lips.

She put a fingertip to his lips. "I know," she said softly. "Believe me, I know. But not here. I think we're being watched."

She shifted her eyes, and without turning his head, Barry followed their direction. He could see a pickup truck parked in the shadows across the street. He could not see who was in it. "Do you know who it is, Brenda?"

"Oh yes. That's Hammer Kearn's truck."

"Hammer. And he is called Hammer . . . ?"

"Because he likes to hammer on people."

"What a delightful county you have here."

They walked back to the inn, and Brenda played with Dog while Barry warmed up the truck. Then he deliberately headed for the Blasingame ruins.

He noticed the pickup truck tagging along behind them, hanging back. Barry switched on his CB and scanner.

". . . toward the Blasingame place," the voice popped out.

"Don't do nothin' stupid with Miss Brenda along, you hear?"

"Ten-four. I ain't gonna do nothin' stupid. I'm jist gonna whup his pansy ass, is all."

Brenda noticed Barry's tight smile. "You find that amusing?"

"Somewhat. Wouldn't you like to see Hammer get his butt hammered on?"

"Suppose there are two of them in that truck, as I suspect there might be?"

"Then two people get hammered on."

"You're very sure of yourself, Barry."

"Very sure."

He drove several miles outside of town, then went down a gravel road and stopped. "Climb down, Brenda. I want a witness to this exercise in futility."

The pickup drove past them, then stopped and backed up; something no professional would have done, for that put the bright lights of Barry's Kenworth shining in their eyes. A dumb move.

"I'm scared, Barry."

"Don't be. Do these people have any redeeming value at all?"

"No," she spoke softly.

"That's good to know."

As the two men approached them, Brenda said, "That's Hammer's cousins. Cuz and Waldo. If it's possible, they're even worse than Hammer."

"Good."

Again, she looked at him very strangely. "Who *are* you, Barry Rivera?"

"You ought to be more careful who you take up company with, Miss Brenda," one of the men drawled. "It ain't fittin' for you to take up with some stranger. Bugger won't like 'at."

"I really don't care what the repulsive bastard likes or dislikes, Cuz. What I do and who I associate with is none of your business."

"Why don't you jist carry your ass on out of here,

Yankee boy?" Waldo told Barry. " 'Fore we decide to kick it plumb out of the county."

Barry laughed at him. "Are you both as ignorant as you appear to be?"

"Haw?" Cuz blurted.

"You sound like a couple of dumb asses." Barry simplified the English language.

"OK, boy," Waldo said. "You asked for it."

Both men came in a rush at Barry. Barry sidestepped and stuck out a boot, tripping Cuz. The man hit the gravel hard, cussing. Barry spun and kicked Waldo on the ass. The man squalled and joined his cousin in cussing. Profanity filled the soft night air.

Cuz came up fast, both hands balled into fists. "I'm a-gonna kill you, boy!" he threatened.

"You heard him say it," Barry spoke to Brenda. "Pure case of self-defense all the way around."

Then he kicked Cuz in the balls. As the man was sinking to the gravel, both hands holding his groin, Barry kicked him in the face, the toe of his boot splintering Cuz's teeth. The man dropped to the gravel, out of the fight.

Barry turned to Waldo, "Now, bully boy. You get to fight one on one. Come on, asshole!"

Waldo stepped in and swung a right; Barry flicked it away and popped the man on the mouth with a left. The blow rocked Waldo, stinging him, bringing blood to his mouth.

For an instant, Waldo's guard was dropped. That was all Barry was waiting for. He buried a right fist into Waldo's belly. The air whooshed out and Waldo doubled over. Putting his hands behind Waldo's head, Barry pulled the head down at the same time he brought his right knee up. Knee and face collided.

The sound of the man's nose breaking was sickeningly loud in the dusty night. Waldo screamed as his nose was crushed. Barry began hammering at the man's kidneys with hard fists, each blow sending shock waves of pain ripping through the man's body. Stepping back, Barry kicked the bully in the face. Waldo's jaw was suddenly pushed over to one side, and he dropped to the gravel, unconscious. Barry walked over to the pickup truck and jerked up on the CB mic, calling for a Dane County sheriff's patrol.

"What are you doing?" Brenda protested. "They'll put you in jail and kill you!"

"I don't think so."

"What's the problem?" a voice came out of the speaker.

"Where are we?" Barry asked Brenda.

"Walnut Ridge Road."

Barry gave the deputy his location and briefly explained what had happened.

"Stay put," the deputy said. "I'm en route."

Cuz groaned and Barry kicked the man on the side of his head, dropping the would-be tough back into unconsciousness. Brenda winced as he kicked the man.

"A decent human being is conditioned to think what you just did is wrong," Brenda spoke. "But I feel no pity for either man."

"Good. Because they damn sure don't deserve any."

Both could see flashing red and blue lights coming up to the intersection fast. The two prowl cars turned off the blacktop and onto the gravel, sliding to a halt.

"Miss Brenda," one of the deputies said. He looked at Barry. "And you are . . . ?"

"Barry Rivera. Brenda and I were driving around

after dinner at the inn. Those two men"—he pointed at the unconscious rednecks on the gravel—"began following us. I finally turned off the blacktop and onto the gravel, where we are now, and got out, asking what they wanted. Brenda climbed down with me. The two became threatening and both of them rushed me. I put them down."

One of the deputies looked at Barry closely. "There ain't a mark on him!"

"They underestimated my ability to defend myself," Barry said.

"Damn sure did," the other deputy muttered. He was uncertain what course of action he should take.

"If there is to be any charges," Brenda said. "Then I am going to file some charges of my own . . . against them!" She pointed at Cuz and Waldo.

The older deputy looked uncomfortable.

"If I am taken into custody," Barry said, "Brenda, I want you to call the FBI and ask for their civil rights division. Advise them what happened and that I was acting in self-defense. Then I want you to call the best attorney in this state, and—"

"Whoa, now!" the older deputy said. "Nobody has said nothin' about you being taken nowhere. Y'all just, ah, go on about your business. Man's got a right to defend hisself. I'll write it up thataway. I don't think Waldo no Cuz will be filin' no charges. Y'all can leave now."

As the Kenworth was rolling once more on the blacktop, the deputy turned to his partner. "Get Mister Maxwell on the horn. I want to nip this thing in the bud—right now!"

Five

"Back there on the road," Brenda said. "You fought like a . . . machine. And I think you enjoyed it, too, didn't you?"

"And you didn't?"

She smiled in the glow of the dash. "I would be lying if I said I didn't. They deserved what they got . . . and more."

"Let's change the subject, Brenda. Why only three years at the university?"

"You have a good memory, Barry." She smiled—a rueful smile. "My . . . parents, and I'm adopted by the way, had been lifelong foes of Maxwell Anson—"

"Had been?"

"They're dead. Accident, so Patrolman Blessing said. Tay Blessing. He's the state cop assigned to this county—one of them anyway." She fell silent.

"And you don't believe it was an accident?"

"Hell, no!" She said it with considerable heat. "It was a set-up job just as surely as there are stars in the sky. Neither of my parents ever touched a drop of liquor, but the report stated they were both highly intoxicated. Said they had been to a party up in Lexington, driving back at three o'clock in the morning. That whole report was nothing but a damned lie!"

"I gather it was an automobile accident?"

"Yes. A very bad one."

"Who would want to kill your parents, Brenda, and why?"

"Maxwell Anson's boys. Any of them; all of them. My dad had barred them from ever coming back to the motel or the restaurant. Said his motel was not going to be used for illicit extramarital activities. Banger, of course, went straight to Big Daddy Anson; he threatened to call in my dad's loans at the bank. Dad told him to try it, and he'd call in the state and federal people. It was a bluff, sure, but it worked for a while, at least.

"But my father went too far with his last move. That was just about three years ago. He and Mother went into Frankfort, to the attorney general's office. Dad said that he had evidence that would stop the Ansons' iron rule over Dane County." She sighed. "Well, it must have been some pretty strong stuff. Before you ask what it was . . . I don't know. Just that Dad and a few others in this county had been quietly collecting evidence against Maxwell Anson and his sons for several years. Personal interviews, signed affidavits, that type of stuff. Well, one of the assistants in the AG's office intercepted the evidence before it got to his boss. The guy took it home with him. His home was broken into—so the story goes. And he was roughed up—so the story goes. A lot of personal things were taken, including the evidence. Three big men in ski masks. The lawyer has since gone into private practice up in Cincinnati. Went in style—so I'm told."

Her laugh was not pleasant. "End of story."

Maybe not, Barry thought. *Maybe the beginning.* "Somebody bought the legal beagle off."

"You got that straight."

"Strange no copies were made of the evidence; I think that's SOP."

"It's what?"

"Standard Operating Procedure."

"If any copies were made, they disappeared. Barry, you don't understand: we're dealing with Maxwell Anson. He's worth half a billion dollars. No one knows for sure. He keeps a very low profile so he can be king of the county. He owns people at the state capital. And I mean literally *owns* them. He owns, in one way or the other, every major business in Dane County. All the big mines, the two big factories, the trucking company. If you speak out against an Anson . . . well, what is it that some religions do? Shun people? Yes. You're shunned. And you lose your job. Maxwell Anson is king. And he'll soon own another business." Her words contained a stinging quality.

He gave her a quick glance. "Let me guess—the Anson Inn."

"Right. And it's so little an amount, but so large when you don't have it."

"The inn isn't profitable?"

"Oh, it's profitable, but my father borrowed money against it to remodel the dining area and kitchen. Now Maxwell refuses to allow me to pay the interest any longer. He wants the principal. And it's all legal."

"How much money are we talking about here?"

She glared at him. "Forget it, Barry!" There was heat in her voice. "I didn't ask to go riding so I could hit you up for a loan."

"I know that." His reply was softly given. "I merely asked, how much?"

"Ten thousand dollars." She turned away, looking

out the side window at the dark landscape as they moved along the blacktop.

Barry laughed.

She shot visual daggers at him. "I'm glad you think it's so funny, Barry. I sure as hell don't see any humor in it."

"I wasn't laughing at you, Brenda." He was silent for a moment. He had been told that no reasonable request would be challenged by Central Command, but to use the number only in an emergency. Now was as good a time as any to check it out. "All right, Brenda. Like you, I'll take a chance. I'll put my trust in you. Your motel is safe . . ." *I think.* "Anson will not touch it."

"Sure," she said sarcastically. "An unemployed truck driver and amateur photographer is going to reach into his pocket and fork over to the little lady ten grand—no strings attached. Sure. Right. Sure you are. Tell me, Mister Big Shot Whoever You Are, what kind of funny cigarettes have you been smoking?"

He grinned. Coming up on a closed filling station, he spotted a public phone. "Come on, Pretty Lady. Let's see if we can't agitate Maxwell Anson just a bit."

She looked at him suspiciously, sighed, then climbed down out of the truck, following him to the phone. "Mister High Finance is now going to call his banker. Stay tuned, folks."

He laughed at her. "What's your personal account number at the bank?"

She had to go back to the truck for her purse. She handed him the card.

"This is the account you want it in?"

"That's a big ten-four."

Again, he laughed at her as he punched out the

numbers to Central Command, charging the call to his card. "This is Dog." He could see her eyes widen. "I want ten thousand dollars sent to this account number in Anson, Kentucky. Bank of Anson." He gave the voice the account number. "First thing in the morning—OK?"

"Whatever you say," the female voice spoke from the other end. "I have been instructed not to question you on any reasonable request."

"Does the government have an agent working in this area?"

"Hang on. I'll bump Elmer. That's the computer." Brenda's eyes were wide and her face pale.

"Affirmative, Dog. Puff."

"The same Puff I worked with in Southeast Asia?"

"There is only one."

"Thanks."

"That's what I'm here for, Dog. Bow-wow." She hung up.

Barry turned to look at a now very startled and pretty woman. "Who in the hell are you?" she blurted.

"Let's just say, for the time being, I'm here to help and leave it at that. Come on."

"What did you boys find in this truck driver's room?" Maxwell Anson asked. He had been told what had happened to Cuz and Waldo; he had not yet enlightened his sons.

"Nuttin'," Banger replied, helping himself to a generous slop of his father's expensive brandy. "He's what he says he is. There ain't no 'pensive clothes 'er boots 'er nuttin' in his room. Sheriff Manville done checked him out on that there computer thing of his'n, and he's clean. He's jist a artsy-fartsy queer truck driver, that's all."

The man looked at each of the sons he'd fathered. He concluded that there wasn't one among them worth a tinker's damn for anything. They were lazy and ignorant, and proud of being ignorant. And he knew that spelled redneck white trash, any way a man wanted to cut it. *But,* he sighed, *I have to accept part of the blame; blood is thicker than water.* To be trite about it. Blood, yes, but concentrated blood, from generations of marrying too closely within the family. Already, they had two idiot monster offspring born from their loins. Maxwell hoped to God that Bugger remained single.

Although he could not for the life of him imagine any woman of quality wanting anything at all to do with him.

"All right," Maxwell said. "Now you listen to me, all of you. Stay away from the man. Stay away from him! Do you understand?"

"Yessuh," they all mush-mouthed.

Look and sound like a bunch of trained apes, the father thought bitterly.

The boys' younger sister, Jennifer, sashayed into the room. "What y'all talkin' about in here?"

"None of your concern, sister," Eddie told her.

"Bet I know." She grinned slyly.

She was greeted by silence.

"That new feller drove into town in that purty rig; takin' pitchers of mansions and sich. Miss Newbury down at the library told me about him this afternoon. She's thrilled—her words. Said he was handsome, too. And" she cut her eyes at Bugger—"talk is that he backed you down real quick."

Bugger got all swoll up like a possum. " 'At's a damn lie!"

"Don't speak to your sister in that tone of voice!" the father cautioned his son. He looked at the girl. "Where'd you hear such talk, girl?"

"It's all over town," she said sullenly, dragging the toe of her tennis shoe on the carpet. Maxwell thought that she did not look a bit coquettish. "Then I heard it down at the dress shop. There was somebody watchin' when brother there got mouthy and then backed down."

"Who heard it?"

"One of the cleanin' ladies."

"Maybe she needs to be taught a lesson, Daddy," Whacker suggested.

Maxwell's eyes were dark with fury. "Goddamn you all! It's your use of force that's got us all in this mess."

"Yessuh," they mush-mouthed.

"Now, did this man back you down, Bugger?"

"He may be a fairy, but he's a bad one," was all that Bugger would say.

"Yes," Maxwell agreed. "He certainly is a bad one." Then he told them all about the fight.

"He whupped Cuz and Waldo all by hisself?" Eddie breathed. "Lard, Lard!"

Maxwell sighed. Then he looked at his daughter, so beautiful, and he idly wondered who she had been screwing that day. Her escapades—and Jane Causy's—were legendary throughout Dane County.

Before he had smartened up, coming to terms with what she was, Jennifer had had two abortions before her fifteenth birthday. Daddy had then put her on the pill. His daughter had the same moral qualities as his sons. None. She would screw anything that wore pants.

And sometimes being male was not necessary; rumors of her lesbian activities had also reached his ears.

Five worthless sons and a whore for a daughter. But in his own way, he did love them all, for he knew they were what he had allowed them to become. Or else the seed had finally turned totally evil.

He chose not to dwell on that.

No, he had given them too much money, too much power, too much of everything except discipline. But damn it, how can a man stand back and allow his sons to be shipped off to prison? The men they had whipped and stomped in fights were nothing more than mine trash and hardscrabble farmers, and the women they had supposedly raped—up until this last incident—probably waved the pussy in their faces.

Maxwell Anson sighed heavily. He'd been doing a lot of that lately. Too much. He poured himself a snifter of brandy and inhaled the fine aroma. Perhaps if his wife had not died; maybe if he had sent his kids off to some tough boarding school. He mentally shook those thoughts away. No point in berating himself on that at this juncture. Nothing could be changed.

"Jennifer, honey," he said. "You run along now. Go play with some of your pretties. I have business to discuss with the boys."

She tossed her head and sailed out of the room, denim-clad derriere swaying from side to side. She gave Bugger a hot look, then showed her displeasure at being dismissed by slamming the study door. Hard.

She'd go play with a pretty, all right, she thought. She'd go get Jane and they'd play with each other. Jane had the prettiest set of titties Jennifer had ever seen. Other than her own pectoral developments, that is.

"Daddy?" Whacker asked. "Why'd you send her out? She was a part of it, too.

"Yes," the father said wearily. "And I cannot for the life of me understand why."

" 'Cause she got her rocks off jist a-watchin'," Eddie bluntly said. "Why, I bet you she cummed—"

"Shut up!" Maxwell screamed. He rubbed his face with his hands. "Kindly . . . please spare me any further details of that night . . . nights. Now you all hear me out." He glared and pointed a finger at each of them. "This time you screwed up. This time, boys, you didn't rape some trashy miner's woman or some bar girl. This time you raped people of quality. *Quality.* Roll that word around on your tongues. Taste it—"

"Oh, we did, Daddy!" Banger blurted. "I just bet you we ate that—"

Maxwell slapped him. Hard. The man's face drained of blood. He was scared shitless of his pappy.

"Keep your filthy talk to yourself. And do not interrupt me again. My father got me out of some bad scrapes back when I was a young buck. But nothing like what I have had to tolerate from all of you. But if you think it's all over and finished—you're wrong. Dead wrong. I thought we might have lucked out. I was wrong. My sources in Washington tell me that we've attracted attention. A Fed is in here."

"The pansy truck driver?" Eddie asked.

"Boy, this Barry Rivera is no pansy. The deputies told me there wasn't a mark on him, yet he beat the shit out of two of the roughest ol' boys in this county. That hundred-and-fifty-thousand-dollar rig he's driving? It's all paid for. Yes—he might be the Fed. And he might be a plant to draw attention away from the real Fed. I don't know. But you stay away from that man."

"Yessuh!" they chanted.

Maxwell turned around, drawing several deep breaths, composing himself. When he again faced his sons, his words were icy cold. "I wish I could take a sabbatical—"

"A whut?" Bugger asked.

"A period of rest," Maxwell said, with more patience than he felt. Away from you cretins. "More or less," he added. "The Rockies, Mexico—anywhere."

"Ever'thang's gonna be alraight, Daddy," Whacker said. "I'd bet my life on it."

"You are," the father said grimly. "And mine, too!"

"I might be crazy for doing this," Barry said. "I have known you for about twenty-four hours, and you're pushing me to level with you. If I did that, Brenda, I would be literally putting my life in your hands."

"Suppose you tell me whatever it is you're going to tell me, and I betray you. What happens then?"

"I kill you!"

"That's blunt enough," she agreed.

Barry looked at her profile, highlighted by the moonlight pouring in through the windows of the truck. "I do trust you, Brenda, but I think it would be unwise for me to level with you entirely. For more than just my own personal safety. I think it would put your life in considerable danger."

She did not take offense. "All right, Barry. If you say so."

"What did you mean about learning your lesson the hard way?"

She grimaced. "You don't know the Anson boys like I do."

"I know them better than you think I do."

She glanced at him. "Yes, you probably do. Whatever you are, you have probably been briefed on what is going on in this county."

Barry said nothing.

"The Anson boys—and their sister—are sadists and perverts."

"Yes, I know. Brenda, what do you know about a rape that supposedly occurred in the county?"

"I thought that might have been it. Nothing, really. Just whispered street talk. And of course you know the husband came in here and then disappeared?"

"So I heard."

"He's dead. His body was probably dumped down some long-forgotten mine shaft. And"—she sighed—"don't believe for an instant that your friend, Toby Kendall, just gave up and pulled out." She fell silent.

"What do you mean? You mean there is *more* mess going on in this county?"

"It's common knowledge—but not talked about—that Dane County has one of the biggest chop shops for rigs in the nation."

"Run, of course, by . . . ?"

"The Anson boys. The rigs are disassembled here and the parts trucked out."

"You would testify to that in a court of law?"

"No, because all I know are rumors."

Now he began to more fully understand why Jackson suggested to come here. Jesus, what a snake pit!

Brenda said, "The Anson boys are . . . warped.

Most people even willing to discuss the family believe the inbreeding of two centuries has finally caught up with them. But they're not to be pitied, Barry. They're cruel and vicious; they like to hurt both people and animals. Anyway, Bugger got his nickname because of his . . . well, how can I put this delicately?"

"You can't. He enjoys anal intercourse."

"Yes. And in doing so, enjoys hurting women. All those thugs, Bugger, Banger, Whacker, Eddie, and Slapper have propositioned me more than once. Whacker and Bugger have even offered to show me their . . . equipment, shall we say, and told me what they would like to do. It was a little more than gross, I assure you."

"I can imagine."

She shook her head. "Not unless you're a woman, you can't. Maybe a certain type of woman is turned on by that sort of thing. They must be the epitome of trash."

"You said you were adopted. Any idea of your real parents?"

Again, she shook her head. "Not a clue. I've never been one of those who was terribly interested in finding out. I think that is probably the best attitude to take."

Barry agreed with her.

"I think I want to go back to the inn, Barry. It's been an eventful night, to say the least."

"I thought I would bring this deposit slip out to you personally, Miss Brenda," Maxwell Anson said. "And to congratulate you on your very good fortune."

"Thank you." She looked at the deposit slip. Ten thousand dollars had been transferred to her checking account. She felt giddy with relief. "I'll pay off my note now, Mister Anson. If that is all right with you."

"That would be fine, Miss Brenda."

She wrote him a check for the amount, handing it to him with a smile. "You will see that my note is sent to me marked paid in full, Mister Anson?"

"Promptly, Miss Brenda." He smiled, but his curving of the lips was void of any well-meaning.

They stood at the front desk of the Anson Inn, looking at each other for a few seconds. Brenda's dislike of the man bordered on black hate. She decided to needle him. "I've decided to change the name of the inn, Mister Anson."

"Oh? And to what, Miss Brenda?"

"The Rivera Inn."

He struggled to maintain control. His eyes narrowed and his lips compressed. Finally he managed to smile. "That is certainly your option."

"Yes. Is there anything else, Mister Anson?"

"To someone who does not know money, Miss Brenda, ten thousand dollars is a lot of money. In reality, it is very little."

"Then why were you pressuring me to pay it off so quickly?" she challenged.

"Just good business practice, Miss Brenda." He wondered where she had gotten the money. Wondered if she had gotten it from Sol Wiseman. She and the Jew were friends. He dismissed that. Wiseman walked a thin line in Dane County, but wouldn't be that stupid.

"Perhaps there is more where that came from?" Brenda again stuck the needle to him.

The ruler of Dane County and the father of fools wore a puzzled look on his face. "Yes," he said softly.

"I would imagine there is. And I cannot help but wonder what you're paying for it."

She understood the not-too-subtle nuance, but she was not going to allow him the satisfaction of making her angry. "As long as I know it's honest and ethical, Mister Anson, that's all that matters. I'm quite sure you are familiar with those words, aren't you?"

"Oh, quite, Miss Brenda. That's the way I conduct all my business."

"Of course, Mister Anson. Of course. I never dreamed otherwise."

They shared smiles—about like a mongoose gazing at a cobra. "Would you object if I took my morning coffee in your dining room, Miss Brenda?"

"Not at all, sir. I have told you often that you are welcome here at any time."

"But not my sons." It was not put in question form.

She stared at him.

"Are they that bad, Miss Brenda? Are they that uncouth?"

"Mister Anson, your sons—all of them, *all* of them—have, at one time or the other, over the years, propositioned me in the crudest of fashion. They have all suggested perverted sex acts. Bugger knows he is not welcome here; why he comes in is beyond me. But you hear me well, Mister Anson, and advise your sons." She tapped the countertop. "I have a thirty-eight under the counter, and I know how to use it. Not well, but well enough. If any of your trashy sons ever again becomes ugly and profane with me, I will shoot him—or them. I will then ask my attorney to change the trial to another county, and take my chances with a jury stacked with women. Do you understand all that, sir?"

"I believe you'd do it, too, Miss Brenda." This time his smile was genuine, filled with a grudging respect. By God, this was a woman of quality!

"Yes, I do, Mister Anson. I meant every word I just said."

He had to say, "Death threats are against the law, Miss Brenda."

"So is rape and murder, Mister Anson." The words popped out of her mouth before she even gave any thought to what she was saying.

His head jerked up, a lock of carefully brushed hair falling out of place. His eyes were cold, his lips a tight cruel line. "What did you mean by that, Miss Brenda?"

"The coffee shop is that way, sir." She pointed, then turned her back to him, busying herself with check-outs. She heard him walk away, toward the outside. The front door slammed.

Barry had spent the morning shooting scenes of near-incredible beauty, out in the country. He now sat in a shady glade, half-asleep. The sounds of running water roused him. He followed the sound until he reached a sparkling little creek. Kneeling down, he washed his face in the cold water, then froze at the sound of a woman's giggling. It was followed by a high, throaty sexual laugh, then by panting and a woman urging a man on.

He started to turn away from the sound before he caught the sight, to slip back up the bank and leave.

Then he heard the woman call out the man's name, and it froze him in disgust.

He slipped toward the sounds of voices, as silently and as furtively as when he had stalked the enemy in

Southeast Asia. Each practiced step placed only after his eyes had searched the ground for sticks and twigs that might crack or pop and give away his position. Woods animals did not step on sticks or twigs, unless they were panicked, running in fear.

Then the couple came into sight. It was more than disgusting. It was sick and perverted.

"I swear, Bugger brother," Jennifer said. "You sure got a tool on you. I ain't never been able to get enough of it."

"Daddy'll kill us both if he ever finds out," Bugger panted. "I don't thank he'd hold much with me humpin' my own sister."

"Shut up and shove, Bugger!"

Barry turned away, sickened by the sights and sounds of open incest. He wondered if darlin' Jenny had screwed all her brothers. More than likely, he concluded.

"Oh, Gawd, Bugger!" she hollered. "Stay with it—stay with it!"

Barry made his way back to the rushing waters and washed his mouth out with the cold liquid. He washed his hands, wishing he could bathe his entire body—anything to remove the verbal and visual filth he had just witnessed.

Jackson, he thought, *you were wrong when you called this place a reeking cesspool . . . it's a prelude to the pits of Hell!*

Six

"I'm fine, Barry," Brenda said, smiling at him. "Thanks for the loan, and it is a loan, I remind you. But—Barry, what's wrong? You look, well, strange."

He ignored that for the moment. "When will you be off the desk?"

"I cleared out my cash drawer a few minutes ago. I can be ready to turn it over to the night clerk in ten minutes. Barry, what's wrong?"

"I . . . ah, need to talk to you. And you're right; something is very wrong."

"Give me twenty minutes to shower and change, and we'll drive over to Newburg and have dinner there. If that's all right with you," she quickly added. "Newburg is just over the line. Ellen County. The Ellen County sheriff despises the entire Anson clan; Big Daddy's power doesn't reach over there. Sheriff Cody is a good, decent man. Maybe we'll see him tonight."

"I'd . . . ah, rather not be too public, Brenda. If you don't mind."

"I see." She met his eyes. "My, how the plot thickens."

"I'll tap on your door in half an hour. I need to take a very long, very hot shower."

* * *

He told her what he had witnessed that day.

They sat in her small suite of rooms: tiny kitchen, bedroom, bath, and small living room. Comfortable and definitely female.

"Bugger and his *sister!* God, Barry, that is absolutely grotesque."

His grin was forced. "They both seemed to be enjoying it immensely, but I certainly agree with you."

"What do you want to do tonight?"

"Forget dinner; we'll get something later. Let's take a drive out into the country."

They were silent for several miles, Barry driving toward yet another old place he had photographed. He finally broke the silence. "I don't know whether the Anson assholes are into electronic bugging or not, but they damn sure can't bug the great outdoors. We'll talk when we stop." He put a finger to his lips, cautioning her to be silent.

She nodded her understanding.

At the old, once-great house, Barry took a blanket from the sleeper and, walking hand in hand with Brenda, strolled up to the ruins, stark and lonely looking in the moonlight. He spread the blanket and she gracefully sank to the ground. Dog had curled up in the sleeper.

On this night, she had dressed in jeans, denim shirt, and tennis shoes. She looked young and lovely and vulnerable. Just how young Barry did not realize until she sat down and her jeans rose up past her ankles, exposing her socks.

Feeling his age, Barry sighed. But somehow the

sight was refreshing and helped to wash away the disgust he'd felt that afternoon.

He settled down beside her. They could hear the wind softly playing dry sounds in the night: a tune for two.

"There is really very little I can tell you, Brenda. For when I leave here, it's doubtful that you will ever see me again."

He heard her sharp intake of breath. She remained silent.

"Also, if I told you the truth, as I said before, your life would be in great danger. I, ah, really am a truck driver. And I do pull legitimate loads. From time to time. What I do the rest of the time . . . well, before this, ah, operation is over, you'll know. And then you probably won't want anything further to do with me."

"Why don't you let me be the judge of that, Barry?"

"In the end, it will be up to you."

"You and Dog just travel around the country together, huh?"

"That's about it."

"What is your CB handle?"

"Dog."

"You're a professional, Barry. And I don't mean a professional truck driver, although I'm sure you are that, too."

"Yes. I am a professional."

"Cuz and Waldo are both in the hospital here, badly beaten. Yet they didn't put a mark on you. You're very good with your hands."

"And feet."

"What were you in the service?"

"Paratrooper, Ranger, Green Beret." He looked at her. "I thought I told you that? Maybe not."

"I don't want to know any more about you." She lay back, stretching out on the blanket. "Barry?"

He turned his head to look at her. "Brenda."

"I'm right here, waiting."

He found her.

Barry stroked her damp satiny skin, his hands loving the smoothness and feel of her.

All sense of time had been lost for them as they made love on the now rumpled and sweaty blanket. And then came the sweetest moment shared by all lovers: that time after the culmination when they lay in each other's arms and murmured things of no importance except to themselves. No hurried pulling away with mumbled words spoken as if from a preprogrammed robot; no averted eyes or embarrassed moments.

He let his fingers trace downward, over her stomach, then into the still-moist pubic thatch between her slim lovely legs. She stirred and sighed under the gentle strokes of his fingers and opened her legs to his touch. Then closed them, trapping his hand.

They had made love almost frantically, at first, and then dozed under the blanket of stars for an hour. She had awakened him with soft gentle kisses on his face and mouth.

He bent his head and tasted a nipple, feeling it harden between his teeth. After a time, she opened her legs and welcomed him.

And yet another sound joined the night sounds: the steady rhythmic sounds of love.

* * *

"Daddy's all steamed up 'bout Miss Brenda," Eddie told Whacker. "Don't 'member ever seein' him so mad."

"I don't thank she knows nuttin' 'bout it," his brother said. "I thank she was just jabberin' to hear her head rattle. Be that as it may, I shore would like me a taste of Miss Brenda."

"I'd lak me a taste of near'bouts anythin'," Eddie said glumly. "My old woman's on the rag agin."

"Turn her over," Whacker suggested.

"She don't like 'at. Says it goes agin what's taught in the Good Book."

"Damn! Is Jodie back holy-rollin' agin? I thought you'd done slapped all that crap outta her?"

"Hell, no! Now she's got the oldest kids talkin' 'bout the layin' on of hands and tongues and all that other shit. She's done blessed ever'thang in the house 'cept my pecker."

"What y'all talkin' about?" Jennifer asked, stepping out onto the porch of the great mansion of one Maxwell Anson. Maxwell had gone visiting for the night.

"Preachin', prayin', and pussy!" Whacker grinned at his sister.

"Y'all might know something about the latter, boys," she said. "But y'all don't know nuttin' about the first two."

"I got me an idee," Eddie said. "How 'bout some brown sugar for tonight?"

"Who?"

"Willie Jefferson's little high yeller gal, Lisa Mae. How far behind is Will to you?"

"A bunch."

"I wanna watch!" Jennifer hopped up and down. "Me and Jane wanna watch it all, boys!"

Eddie laughed. "Hell's fire, Jenny. You just wanna go with us to see Willie's retarded boy, that's all."

" 'At's a damn lie!" But she knew it wasn't. Not really. She'd heard talk that Willie's silly boy had been entertaining several white ladies in the county. That he had him a pecker that was out of this world, and could stay with you until you nearly died.

"How old is Lisa Mae?" Whacker asked.

"Oh, twelve, I reckon. Old enough. She be virgin stuff, for shore."

"Shit!" Jennifer drawled. "Don't you believe that."

And while Barry and Brenda were sharing a few moments of genuine, caring, feeling emotion, members of the Anson family were busy tugging at the invisible ropes that would soon bring down the curtain on the Ansons' rule of terror and brutality in Dane County.

"Willie," his wife warned him. "You're talking dangerous nonsense."

He stared at her. "No, I ain't. And you know it. I'm talkin' about Maxwell Anson's high-handed tactics and his white-trash sons and whore daughter. That's who I'm talkin' about."

"Willie!" she gasped, looking around her, frightened that even in her own home someone might be listening.

The husband turned his head in disgust and shame. "Look at you," he spoke softly. "Afraid in your own home. Pitiful. Thank God, we ain't got but three more young'uns to get gone from the nest. Well, two, really. The Good Lord seen fit to give us a burden for the rest of our lives with Tate."

"That's blasphemy, Willie!" his wife hissed.

"No, it ain't, Mother. It's the truth, and you know it. The boy's not right in the head. I love him, and I'll care for him and protect him, but he's a fool and you know it. God don't strike me dead for sayin' this, but the boy is nothin' but a walkin' around, grinnin' hard-on. If his brains was the size of his pecker, he'd be a genius."

Despite her fear of what her husband was saying, and the knowledge that he was mixed up in some secret organization of blacks and whites in Dane County, she had to smother a giggle. "Well, you might say he come by it natural."

Willie returned her smile. "Thank you, Mother, but you can go to Hell for lyin'." They laughed, and then Willie sobered. "Jean, I don't worry about; she's too young. But Lisa Mae's got me tossin' and turnin' at night, worryin'."

"There ain't no cause for that, Willie. Lisa Mae is a good girl!"

"I know she is, but she's buddin' out. And I don't know how far behind I am with my payments to Whacker and Eddie. I know I'm too far to ever catch up."

Shirley Jefferson hissed her fear and outrage. "They wouldn't do that!"

"Shit, woman! What are you sayin'? They damn sure would. And has lots of times—all over the county. Don't you never listen to nobody?"

"All that's just talk."

"Oh, Shirley! Tighten up, girl! Them Anson boys is nothin' but pure white trash. They'd stick it in a snake if someone would hold it still long enough. Why you think I been pacin' the floor at night?"

Panic leaped into the woman's eyes. She clutched

at her apron. "Then we gotta send her off somewheres; get her away from here. We got no choice, Willie."

The husband sighed. "Sure, Momma, sure. I'll just write me out a check in the mornin' for two or three thousand; take it to the bank and see if they'll cash it. Get us all out of this hellhole. Shit, baby! If boat rides on the big river was two bits a throw, all I could do is run up and down the bank hollerin', Ain't that cheap!"

She said nothing in rebuttal. She knew it was the truth he spoke. They were busted.

"County is fixin' to blow wide open, Shirley. Violence is gonna flare like wildfire. I just hope it comes in time."

The phone rang. Willie looked at it, puzzled. "I thought the phone company come and turned that thing off?"

Shirley looked embarrassed and would not meet her husband's gaze. "I . . . my sister sent us the money. Some money."

"Goddammit!" Willie slammed a work-hardened hand down on the table, rattling the salt and pepper shakers and jingling the spoons in the Mason jar. "I told you, by God—"

"Answer the phone, Willie!" The woman stood her ground.

Willie jerked up the receiver.

"Henry here, Willie," the voice sprang into his head. "They're comin'. Whacker, Eddie, Jennifer, and some other white woman. Be there in about five minutes. Just passed my place. Move, man, get Lisa Mae in the timber."

"I—she's in bed, Henry." There was a spreading

sick feeling in the pit of Willie's stomach. "No time. At least Jean's spendin' the night at a friend's house. Thank God. What's them white women doin' with the boys?"

"You know, Willie. Think about it. I tried to warn you that Tate's been messin' with white women in the valley. Run, man!" The line went dead.

"Oh, Jesus Lord!" Willie moaned, replacing the receiver in the cradle. "Not Tate."

"What about Tate?" his wife asked, her knuckles white from gripping the edge of the kitchen table. "Who's comin' out here tonight?"

"The Anson boys. Jennifer's with them. And some other white lady. Not no lady. Oh, Lord!"

"What's them women want out here?"

"Hell, Shirley . . . they probably want some of Tate. It has to be Mister Causy's daughter, Jane."

Car lights flashed on the side of the unpainted house; tires crunched on gravel. Car doors opened and thudded closed.

"I tried and tried to figure out a way to pay them boys," Willie said, his voice containing a moan. "Too late now."

Shirley started crying.

"Willie Jefferson!" Whacker's voice was hard and demanding. "Get out here, boy."

Willie glanced at his wife. "Get Lisa Mae out of bed. Get her into the timber."

The woman seemed powerless to move. "This can't be happenin'. I don't believe it. This went out twenty-five years ago."

"Not in Dane County, it didn't," Willie reminded her. "Move, Mother." He stepped out onto the porch. "What do you want, Whacker?"

"Mister Whacker, *sir!* Don't you get uppity with me, boy!" Whacker popped the words at him.

"Yassuh," Willie mush-mouthed. Anything to buy a little time.

" 'At's better, boy," Eddie said. "We come out here to collect the back payments you owe Whacker. You know how much it is, so git it."

"Ain't got it, Mister Eddie. Cain't get it, neither. You'll jist have to wait."

"Don't you tell me what I have to do! I said to git the money, so by God, you git it."

"And I said I ain't got it!" Willie told him. "And I ain't never gonna have it as long as folks keep chargin' ten for five."

"Now, now," Whacker said soothingly, stepping between his brother and Willie. "Let's not get all worked up here. How much you owe me, Willie?"

Willie mumbled the amount.

"I cain't hear you, boy. Speak up to me, Willie."

"I said you know how much it is, Whacker!" Willie's eyes flashed in the summer's night. He knew he was getting awfully close to the danger line.

"*Mister* Whacker, sir!" Whacker shouted. "Say it, boy!"

"Yassuh, Mister Whacker, suh." Willie's shoulders slumped in defeat. Years of conditioning took over and pushed pride out of the way.

"And you ain't got the money—is that right, Willie?"

"Nosuh, Mister Whacker, I shore don't have the money."

"What you plan on doin' about it, then?"

"Don't know, Mister Whacker."

"Well, I thank we best jaw on it some. We can work

somethin' out, Willie." Whacker smiled slyly. "Where's that fool boy of your'n?"

"He's around, I reckon. He's shy. Don't like to come around other folks much."

"Git him."

Wild, almost uncontrollable thoughts leaped into Willie's head: his shotgun in the closet, his deer rifle beside it, the pistol in the nightstand—was it loaded? The knife in its scabbard.

But Willie fought them all away. He knew that if harm was to come to an Anson . . . well, folks had disappeared, been lynched, beat, and stomped to death for a lot less than that.

But it wasn't right. Wasn't nothing about it right. He'd heard about some federal man who was supposed to be in the county. Folks said it was that hard-eyed man who drove that big eighteen-wheeler. But one man, one man against the Ansons? Didn't seem reasonable.

"Ohhh, Tate," Willie called. "Tate, child!"

"Ohhh, Daddy!" the young man called from behind the house, where he'd been hiding, watching, fearfully listening to the exchange. There was fear in his father's voice, and the young man didn't understand that.

"You come on around to the front, boy. Gentlemans wants to see you."

The teenager shuffled forward, standing at the edge of the porch. There was a vacant look in his eyes, a slight slackness to his mouth. He was huge for his age, with heavily muscled arms and shoulders, a barrel chest. His shirt and jeans were too small for him.

Eddie said, "You raight sure that boy ain't dangerous, Willie?"

"He as gentle as a lamb, Mister Eddie. Ain't never hurt nobody or nuttin'. Loves animals and people. Course, there ain't nobody ever hurt him, either."

"Take your word for that," Eddie replied, looking at Tate. He looked back at Willie. "That barn yonder got lights?"

"Yassuh."

"Boy," Eddie said to Tate. "You go over by the car. Them white ladies tell you what they want. You do what they say, now, you hear?"

Tate grinned foolishly, and bobbed his head up and down. "Yassuh, I will." He walked off toward the car and the . . . ladies.

"I just bet he will." Whacker punched his brother in the ribs. "He's a plumb fool but he knows what his pecker's there for."

Both men got a good laugh out of that. Willie stood helplessly on the front porch, a dozen plans forming in his head. He rejected them all as soon as he thought of them.

Whacker reached into his back pocket and pulled out a pint of whiskey. "Now then, Willie, we'll have a drink and then git down to business." He held out the bottle. "Here, boy, take yourself a good swaller of that. Puts lead in your pencil."

"I don't drink, suh."

Whacker flushed in the night. "Gawddamn you, boy! When I tell you to take a drink of whiskey, you take a drink! Now you understand all that, boy?"

"Yasshuh." Willie stepped off the porch and took the offered bottle of hooch.

The sounds of Jennifer and Jane giggling drifted to the men.

"Got plenty more where that came from, boy," Eddie said. "Plenty more. Hell, we jist might have ourselves a party night."

Both white men laughed. Willie did not.

Willie could hear his wife weeping in the house. He knew, with a sinking feeling in his guts, that she had not taken Lisa Mae and run.

Seven

"What's the matter, Barry. I felt you drawing away from me a minute ago."

Barry sat up. The night had cooled and they now were fully dressed. "A slight feeling of guilt, I suppose. I'm not doing what I came here to do."

"I don't want to pursue that." She snuggled closer to him. "How old are you, Barry?"

"Too old for you."

She giggled. "Cradle robber."

"I hesitate to ask your age, tender though it may be."

"I am an old lady of almost twenty-five who just happens to enjoy the company of a slightly older man. And you know what, old man?" He shook his head solemnly. "I don't care. And might I add, for a man of your advanced years, you are the horniest dude I have ever known."

"Long time between women."

"Why? Were you in prison?"

"No. A hospital. And don't ask any more questions about it. Please," he added.

"Ten-four."

He had to laugh at that.

"I don't want this to end, Barry."

"But it will. Accept that. I can't believe you don't have any serious boyfriends."

"But it's true. You have no serious lady friend?"

"No. I was married. I lost my wife."

She did not pursue that. She lay back on the blanket and gazed up at the stars. "They seem so close."

"That's not all that's close this night."

"What do you mean?"

"Trouble."

" 'At's right, Willie," Whacker said. "Finish the bottle. Go ahead, boy. We got lots more."

Not a drinking man, Willie swayed on his feet, dropping the empty pint bottle on the ground. "Don't want no more, suh." He slurred the words.

"Sure you do, Willie." Eddie snapped the seal on another pint of booze. He handed the bottle to Willie. "Take a big drink, boy."

Willie gulped down a mouthful of the fiery amber liquid. It hit his stomach like a small explosion. He fought to keep from puking.

"All right, Willie," Whacker said. "Time we got down to business. Where's that daughter of your'n this night?"

"Which one?"

"Lisa Mae."

"In the house. She's sleepin'."

"Git 'er."

"What for?"

"Time for you to start payin' off your obligation to us, boy. Now don't ask no questions. You just git her."

Willie shook his head. "No, suh; ain't gonna do it. She ain't but twelve."

"Gawddamn you, Willie!" Whacker shouted. "Don't

tell me what you is or ain't gonna do. You gonna do whatever the hell it is I tell you to do. Now you git that kid of your'n out here."

Willie shook his head. "No, suh. Have to pay my debt some other way. Please, Mister Whacker, I'm beggin' you to don't do this thing. It ain't right."

Whacker laughed at him, large and cruel in the night. "Well, I'll tell you what, Willie. You git down on your hands and knees and beg me. Then maybe I'll change my mind."

Willie knew raw hatred then, and the urge to kill was strong in him. It wasn't just that these Anson boys did this to black people; they did it to whites as well. It was time, Willie thought, time for the whites and blacks of the county to come out of the darkness and stand up.

But first there was Lisa Mae to think of. He swallowed his pride and dropped down to the ground on his knees. "Please, Mister Whacker. I'm doin' like you asked. I'm beggin'. Don't hurt my girl."

Eddie licked his lips. "Are you tryin' to tell us your kid ain't never been pronged?"

"Yessuh."

"That'd make it even better," Whacker said. He rubbed his crotch. "Shit, I'm gettin' a boner just thinkin' about it."

Willie shook his head, trying to clear away the cobwebs from the alcohol. He knew it was hopeless; but he had to try. He was not going to allow this to happen. He'd die first.

He rose to one knee. "You're not gonna hurt my little girl, Whacker."

"*Mister* Whacker!"

"Fuck you!" Willie said, then leaped at the bigger

and younger man. Willie's charge knocked Whacker and sent him sprawling. Willie got in one good punch to Whacker's jaw before Eddie kicked him off his brother.

Rolling, Whacker jumped to his feet and hit Willie in the mouth, knocking him down. He kicked Willie in the stomach. The man's head slammed against the wooden porch steps. He moaned once and then was still.

Whacker ran up onto the porch and hit the door with a heavy shoulder, splintering it. He stepped inside and ripped the phone from the woman's hand. "Who you callin', bitch?"

"No—nobody, Mister Whacker."

"You're a damn liar!" He slapped her, sending her sprawling with a back hand. He held the phone to his ear. Nothing but a hum. She had not had time to dial. The woman slumped to the linoleum floor, weeping.

Whacker turned to his brother. "Drag Willie in here. Tie him up to that overhang yonder. Tie him up good now. Loop a noose 'round his neck; give him enough slack so's he can breathe, but tight enough so's he'll know he chokes if he tries to fight it." He looked down at the woman. "Git Lisa Mae out here, woman."

She shook her head. Whacker kicked her savagely on the thigh. She cried out in pain.

Whacker strode angrily to a closed door and kicked it open. A young girl sat huddled and scared on the bed. Whacker grinned at her. "Git out here, yeller gal. And don't give me no sass about it, either."

The girl, numb with fear, scooted off the bed and eased toward Whacker, standing in the door. He grabbed her and fondled her budding breasts.

Shirley Jefferson put her cheek against the coolness of the floor and wept as her husband was dragged in and tied up, his toes just touching the floor. The noose around his neck was tightened, his hands tied behind his back.

"Shuck outta that nightgown, girl," Whacker told the child. Her eyes were big and round and frightened. "Lemme see the snatch."

Jane Causy looked at the young man standing naked under the hanging lightbulb in the small barn. "He's a fool!" she summed up.

"Sure he is," Jennifer agreed. "I don't know about you, but I didn't come out here to check his I.Q."

The two young women, both in their early twenties, had been friends almost since birth. Jane's father was the second in command of Maxwell Anson's vast empire; he was gone most of the time, overseeing and manipulating the huge interests. Jane, like Jennifer, had been kicked out of a dozen colleges before both men, widowers, realized their daughters were not interested in any type of education—except what a man could do for them.

Then they did what many parents do. They gave up on their kids.

"Gawd!" Jane hissed. "He's a big sucker, ain't he? You sure he ain't dangerous?"

"Hell fire, Jane! You think we the only women that stud services—black and white. You do, and you're a fool. Get over yonder on the hay, boy," she ordered. "Let's see what you can do."

Tate grinned and moved toward the hay pile. He

knew what they wanted, and he knew that was one of the few things he could do well.

"Who goes first?" Jane asked.

"Me!" Jennifer said. She looked at Tate. "No kissin', boy. You understand that?"

He nodded his head. They all said the same, but after a few minutes, they always forgot it.

"And you ever say anythang about this evenin', to anybody, my brothers will kill you. You understand all that?"

Tate nodded. He'd heard it all before. It was boring. They all said the same thing.

"Slap her agin," Whacker told Eddie. "And hold her down, damn it!"

"I'm tryin', damn it!" He slapped the child. "It's worser than tryin' to grab holt of an eel." He slapped her again. She sobbed once and then lay still on the floor.

"I'll kill you, Whacker!" Willie said hoarsely, the rope biting at his neck. "If there is a God in Heaven, I'll kill you both for this."

Whacker grinned at him. "How come it is that you're black as a wore-out inner tube, all the rest of your kids is black as boot polish, but Lisa Mae's a yeller gal? Your wife been steppin' over your neighbor's woodpile, maybe?"

"White-trash son of a bitch!" Willie cussed him.

Whacker thought it all funny. "You hear 'at, Eddie? Coon here is callin' you and me white trash. Have mercy!"

"Maybe after we have our fun, we ought to cut him; turn him into a geldin'?"

"You better kill me, boys," Willie warned. " 'Cause you done gone too far this time."

"Don't push your luck, nigger." Whacker's words held an ugly note of warning. "Push us some more, and we just might oblige you."

"Whacker?" Eddie called, kneeling between the girl's legs. Lisa was sobbing. "We got us a cherry. Praise the Lord!"

"Git outta the way. I git to bust it!"

Soon Lisa Mae's screaming joined the shrieking and hollering from the barn.

One vastly differed from the other.

"We're being watched," Barry said softly, his words just a whisper in the night. "Get up and walk slowly toward the truck."

"Who?"

"I don't know." His fingers found the butt of the Woodsman in his belt.

"We don't mean no harm, mister," the voice came from the creek bank to their left. "And we ain't been here long, so we ain't been listenin' to nothin' you and Miss Brenda been sayin' or doin'—whatever it might have been."

Barry heard Brenda's intake of breath. Sharp. "Adam Wallace!" she called. "Is that you, boy?"

"Yes'um, Miss Brenda. It is."

"Who is it?" Barry asked.

"I went to school with Adam, Barry. He used to work for Anson's Independent Mine Company. Got fired. Him and a lot of other men. Anson called them troublemakers."

"The mine nonunion?"

"Bet on that. No unions of any kind in Dane County. Low wages is the standard."

A tight knot of men appeared from the line of timber running alongside the creek. As they drew nearer, Barry could see it was a group of blacks and whites.

One of the younger white men stepped forward, extending his hand. Brenda took it. "Adam!" Her voice was cool. "You want to explain all of this, please?"

"Yes'um. We meet once a week. Nearby. Heard y'all talkin', seen the light reflect off his rig." He looked at Barry. "Talk is there's a government man workin' this area; gatherin' evidence on Big Daddy Anson. You him?"

Barry shook his head. "No, I'm not, Adam." Barry shook the offered hand. "I assure you, I am not that government man."

Brenda picked up on *that*.

"Anson and Sheriff Manville don't think thataway. They're awful interested in you."

"They're wasting their time."

"Uh-huh." The reply indicated the miner didn't believe him either.

Barry looked more closely at the group of men. He could see pistols stuck behind a lot of belts. Not going to take much to set off one hell of an explosion in this county.

"You men are armed!" Brenda noticed the guns.

"Yes'um. It's best nowadays. Lots of trouble in this county."

Brenda and Barry waited for the man to elaborate.

Adam sighed. "You may as well know. Both of you. Whacker and Eddie and that whore sister of theirs—excuse me, Miss Brenda—and that slut Jane Causy is over to Willie Jefferson's place."

"Why?" she asked.

Adam got suddenly embarrassed. "Well . . . maybe you ain't heard what them Anson boys do, Brenda; and maybe you ain't heard about young Tate, neither."

"What about Tate?" she asked. "Isn't he the one who is mentally retarded?"

"Yes'um. But—ah—well. I can't proper say this in front of you, Miss Brenda."

Brenda lost her patience. She had had quite enough of "yes-ums" and "ma'ams" for one evening. "Adam Wallace! I am a growed-up woman." She slipped easily back into the mountain dialect. "And you don't see no halo 'round my head, do you? So speak your piece, boy!"

Barry struggled to hide his grin.

Adam shuffled his booted feet. "Well, Brenda, Tate's built up right well."

"I have heard he's a very muscular young man, yes. So what about it? Is he being used as forced labor or something like that?"

"Uh . . . ?" Adam gave Barry a desperate look for help.

"He's trying to tell you, as tactfully as possible, Brenda"—Barry's tone was dry—"that this Tate boy is amply endowed in the penis department."

She looked at him. "Oh!"

"Fellow sure talks funny," someone in the crowd muttered.

"Oh!" Brenda said, louder. "You mean they are using that poor boy—" She bit it off.

Adam smiled at Barry. "Obliged, mister. But 'amply endowed' is puttin' it mild. Young Tate services a lot of women in this area. Of all colors. We figure that

Jenny and Jane went over there to—use his services while Whacker and Eddie collects their debt from Willie—in a manner of speaking, that is."

"Lisa Mae isn't but twelve, Miss Brenda," a black man said. "She's buddin' out right well; but small for her age. I don't know if you ever heard what happened to Johnny Springer's little girl, Betsy, did you, ma'am?"

"I don't know what you're talking about, Robert." Brenda looked at him. "Nor what you just tried to say, Adam. What about the Springer girl?"

But Robert just shook his head. "No, ma'am. Ain't my place to say nothin' like that in front of a good woman."

"Robert!" Brenda stamped her foot. "Now you stop this foolishness. You've known me since the day I was born!"

But Robert just shook his head again.

"The Anson boys like to have sex with young girls," Barry said. "Is that it, Adam?"

Adam's sigh was painful. Barry looked at the tight faces of the men. Angry faces. Ugly with rage and hate.

"You see, Brenda, the Anson boys, all of them, like to get families in debt to them. 'Specially families with girls. Then when they can't pay the loans—and nobody can the way they're set up—well, the Anson boys take up the slack with the young girls. Or the man's wife, as the case may be."

"That is sick and totally disgusting!" Brenda spat out the words. "Depraved!"

"Yes'um," Adam agreed.

"And *illegal!*" she shouted.

Barry kept his mouth shut.

"Yes'um. And that's what your daddy had when he sent that stuff over to the state attorney general's office. Signed papers from folks who'd had kids . . . well, used. And a whole bunch of other stuff as well. But"—he shrugged—"you see how far that went."

Another man said, "Betsy still ain't got over what Banger and Mayor Bradley done to her. Oh, Big Daddy Anson picked up all the bills and such, but Betsy wasn't just hurt physically." He tapped the side of his head. "They messed up her mind, too."

"I knew it was bad," Brenda muttered. "But I had no idea it was this bad." She shook her head. "How can this be happening? It's—" She could not find the words.

"Things is fixin' to pop around here," Adam told them. "Black and white is solid together on this. And when it does . . . well, that's why we was hopin' your fellow here was that government man. In a way we was."

Barry felt that the government man—and he didn't think it was Puff, for Puff was a gun, period—had best keep his head down and stay low. These mountain men had given up on any legal methods of correcting the wrongs. They were going to do it their way.

"May I ask when all this is going to take place, Adam?" Brenda looked at him.

The man shook his head. "Can't tell you that. Soon, though. We'll try to warn you folks in time. Keep your heads down when it blows. Folks around here have had a gut-full of the Ansons. I'm afraid it's going to be bloody."

Barry noticed his dialect came and went at will. He got the impression that Adam had had more education than he let on.

And that did not surprise him at all. He had friends in south Louisiana who held Ph.D.s and talked as though they didn't have enough sense to tie their own shoes.

"You've completely given up doing this in any legal manner?" Barry asked the crowd.

A dozen sets of eyes swung silently toward him. "We told you," a man spoke from out of the crowd. "Yeah, we thought on it a lot. Mister Hooks, Brenda's father, he tried it legal. Got him killed. And he hadn't been the only one dead.

"You got to understand something: all them Anson boys make folks sign papers when they loan money. The interest rates are legal ones. The five-for-ten rate is based on a handshake. And a lot of the women they . . . use won't come forward and make charges agin the boys. Shamed, I suppose. But even if they did, it wouldn't do no good. The sheriff's in Anson's pocket, and so is the DA and the judge. So what's the point? And some of the men get stomped on pretty good; turns a man edgy. You just don't understand; hard for an outsider, I know that. It's sad, mister. Real sad."

"Sad is not the word I would use," Brenda said heatedly.

Adam smiled. "Yes'um. I can tell you, we've used all sorts of words in talkin' about the Ansons. This government man, so we heard, was called in about a month ago; there may be more than one. Don't really know. And there's somethin' about a rape and murder that maybe happened around here. Can't get a good fix on that rumor."

Barry remained impassive.

"But there're other rumors that he's been here over

a year; maybe longer. That's the problem. We just don't know."

"Don't do anything you men can be sent to prison for," Brenda warned the crowd.

"We're in prison, Brenda." Adam's words were slow but harshly spoken. "And you know it. Everyone in Dane County. It's just that there ain't no iron bars and stone walls, that's all."

The crowd of men nodded their heads in agreement. And Barry knew the time for talking was just about gone. These men were ready to do their talking with guns. Mountain way. As if on a silent signal, the crowd slowly turned and disappeared into the darkness.

Just sit back, Barry cautioned himself. *Don't jump in until you're pushed.* But he knew he was not the sort of man to do that. "The pot is boiling, almost ready to explode. And it's going to be bad."

"That's true, Barry."

"If we could ice the ringleader, that might stop it."

"Ice?" She looked at him.

"Kill him!"

"We'll cut off here," the tanned, hard-eyed man said to his traveling companions. They were as tough looking as he. "See my brother, Sol. Haven't seen him in several years."

"That who you bought the presents for, Colonel?"

"Yes. And for his children. Esther and Ruth."

"If we get stopped and searched, we're going to raise some eyebrows with these weapons we're carrying," the colonel was told.

"I don't think so. One phone call will straighten it

all out. The weapons were declared when we entered the country; we're here by invitation from the departments of State and Defense. Our next demonstration is at Fort Knox. No, we're legal. We'll spend the night with Sol and be on our way." He smiled. "Have you ever eaten grits, Samuel?"

"Grits? What the hell is that?"

The colonel laughed. "Welcome to the South, men. Oh, I think you men will enjoy your visit here. Anson is a peaceful little town."

"Beats the hell out of the Gaza Strip," the third man muttered.

Eight

The child had been beaten into submission. Blood leaked from her mouth where Eddie had clubbed her with his fists. She was now, mercifully, unconscious.

"It ain't no fun no more," Eddie bitched, hitching up his jeans. "You got all the good out of her, Whacker."

"Told you not to beat on her so much." He looked at Lisa Mae. "She ain't dead, is she?"

"Naw."

Willie hung from his ropes and cursed them, the profanity rolling from his mouth in waves.

Whacker glared at the man. "Go git us a club, Eddie. I reckon it's time we taught Willie his place."

"Leave him alone!" Shirley screamed.

She got a kick in the stomach for saying that. She huddled in a ball on the floor, gagging. Eddie returned with a broken axe handle.

"That'll do just fine," Whacker said, taking the axe handle. He viciously brought the wood down on Willie's back.

Willie screamed as the wood tore his flesh and bruised his muscle. Whacker jabbed him several times in the stomach, each short, brutal jab harder than the one before. Willie felt something give within him.

"Now you tell me what it is you was gonna do to us, Willie?"

"Kill you!" the man gasped.

Whacker hit him again. He kicked him in the groin and smashed his fists against the man's mouth and hammered him in the stomach. Willie passed out from the pain.

There was a strange look in Whacker's eyes. The torturers of the Inquisition must have worn the same look.

Whacker tossed a bucket of water onto Willie, reviving him.

"You wanna see your woman beat?"

Willie shook his head.

"You got the words in your head, Willie. The proper words to say to white people. So say 'em."

Willie humbled himself. Anything to get these men gone and Lisa Mae to a doctor. "I apologize for them things I said to you and Mister Eddie." The words were bitter on his tongue. "You was right in beatin' me. I ain't never gonna cause you no more trouble." *Just kill your trash ass,* he thought.

"Nothin' happened this night, did it, Willie?" Whacker prompted the man.

"No, suh. Nothin' at all."

"And the next time we come around, you ain't gonna kick up no fuss about your kid, is you, Willie?"

"No, suh." But if looks could kill.

Eddie laughed. "A man's just got to teach 'em their place ever' now and then." He looked at Shirley. "You don't move for ten minutes after we're gone from here, you understand that?"

"Yes, suh," she said through her tears.

Whacker jerked the phone cord loose and tossed

the phone to the floor. "We be goin' now. You don't move till we long gone, you hear?"

"Yes, suh," she said.

"Hey!" Eddie said. "I just had me a thought."

"What?"

"Don't the Good Book say it's better to give than to receive?"

"Yeah, somethin' like that."

"Well, Tate been givin' for better than a hour now." He looked at Shirley. "You oughta be right proud of your boy."

Whacker and Eddie thought that amusing. They laughed and spat on the floor.

Lucas Webster, pastor of the Pine Creek MB Church, jacked a round into the chamber of his .30-30. His wife looked at him through eyes that reflected love and fear.

"Don't do this, Lucas!" she pleaded. "If not for me, think of the kids."

"Stay out of it, Nina. I'm goin' over to the Jeffersons. Somethin's wrong. They ain't answerin' the phone."

"Maybe it's out of order?" she suggested hopefully.

"Wasn't a couple of hours ago."

"It's too soon, Lucas."

"Our kind all thought like that, Nina, we'd still be pickin' cotton under a bullwhip. I'm gonna gather up a few men, then we'll decide if it's time. You still don't understand, do you?" She shook her head. "Nina, this is not a black and white issue. This is blacks and whites workin' together to cure a mutual wrong. A century's old evil in this county. I'm a black man, and I'll be leading white *and* black men. They picked me, Nina. Took a show of hands and it was unanimous. That is quite a responsibility."

His wife began to cry, the tears streaking her face, dripping down to the front of her dress. "You know what that Hammer Kearn told you, Lucas; said you cause any more trouble in this county, and he'd kill you personal. Lucas, you behave as if this is some sort of holy mission."

"Maybe it is, Nina. And maybe I'll fall in battle. I fell in Korea and got up and kept on fightin' on that ridge. And right here"—he pointed above the fireplace—"is my Silver Star to prove it. But this fight is just as important as that one—maybe more. Take down the Bible and read it when I leave, Nina. Some experts say, and I believe, that Solomon wrote Ecclesiastes—"

"You ain't Solomon," she bluntly reminded him. "And you're fifty-three years old."

He ignored her interruption. ". . . and Solomon wrote: To every thing there is a season, and a time to every purpose under the Heaven: a time to kill, and a time to heal; a time to break down, and a time to build up."

His wife glared at him. "And why don't you repeat the next verse, Mister Hotshot Preacher! A time to weep, and a time to laugh; a time to mourn, and a time to dance!"

"You well might weep and mourn," he said softly. "And yet, you might laugh and dance. We'll just have to wait and see. If a hundred die so ten thousand can be free . . . that's fine with me. But just remember this: I love you. Whatever happens, I love you."

He rose from the table and, carrying his rifle,

stepped out onto the porch, softly closing the door behind him. He got into his truck and drove away, up the gravel road.

Dog had left the sleeper and was lying on the floorboards, by Brenda's feet, as the three of them drove slowly back toward town.

"Tell me what you know about the men in the Sheriff Department, Brenda?"

She snorted her disgust. "I trust one of them, Granger Kildare. He's not what he wants people to think."

"I met him; I got the same impression. What do you think he is?"

"I'm not sure. Maybe from the state police; perhaps from the federal government. He stays pretty much to himself. Came here, oh, about two years ago. I get . . . well, peculiar vibes from him. He's nice; but maybe that's it. He's too nice."

"I get the impression he's acting a part."

"Yes, so do I. And there's another person; a man who came in about a week after that rumor of the rape and murder surfaced. He tried to hire on at the mines, but they wouldn't take him. Anson's orders, I guess. His name is Johnny South. He stayed at the inn for a few days, finally found a small furnished house just outside of town."

Barry smiled. *Good ol' Puff.*

"Why are you smiling?"

"Johnny South, huh. God!" He laughed aloud, then sighed. "This is going to get messy. Brenda, Johnny South is one of the names this man uses; I don't know his real name. When we worked together in the Company—the CIA—Johnny and I were about the same age. He uses the code name of Puff."

"What does he do?"

"He kills people."

"For whom?"

"For the government. He's the most dangerous man I have ever seen. Puff can kill with his hands, a rolled-up newspaper, a pencil—anything. Puff is awesome."

"I wonder who sent him here?"

Barry looked at her. "Somebody who doesn't like what's been going on in this county, I would imagine."

Barry caught lights in his mirrors. Some damned jackass was following them with his lights on bright. In Barry's opinion, only an inconsiderate asshole would do something like that. He said as much aloud.

"Can you tell what kind of a car it is?" Brenda asked.

"Pickup. I can't see it well enough to know what kind."

"Is it red?"

"Ahhh . . . yeah. Yeah, it is. And there is another pickup behind that one."

"Kin of Cuz and Waldo in the red truck, probably the other truck, too. I think we're in trouble."

"If they think they're going to give me much trouble with those little pissy trucks they're in, they'd better think again."

Barry caught the spark of a gun and then heard the slug bang into the sleeper. "Sons of bitches!" he cussed, as they came out of a curve and onto a long straight stretch. "Hold it in the road," Barry told Brenda, and before she could protest, he had left his seat and was in the sleeper.

"Barry!"

When he again sat down, taking the wheel, he held an M-10 in his right hand. He dropped a bag of loaded clips on the floorboard back of his feet.

"What is *that?*" Brenda questioned.

"M-10. It speaks with authority."

Another round slammed into the truck. "That does it," Barry muttered.

He pulled off onto the small shoulder of the road. The pickup truck behind him surged forward, coming up fast. Barry had stopped the tractor.

Brenda noticed that he was smiling.

When the pickup truck pulled even with him, Barry leaned out the window and held the trigger back.

The clip emptied of 9mm lead, turning the cab of the pickup into a death wagon. The pickup behind it slammed on its brakes, the driver losing it momentarily, and the truck nosing off the road.

Barry quickly slipped in another clip and began turning the Kenworth around. The pickup truck that was still full of living rednecks had burned rubber backing out of the ditch. Barry shifted and came up swiftly behind the smaller truck. In his headlights, he could see the frightened faces of those in the cab as they turned around to stare, open-mouthed.

"You know them?" Barry asked.

She stared at him. "Don't you feel anything?"

"Yes. Satisfaction. I asked you a question: do you know them?"

"They work for the Anson family."

"What kind of people are they?"

She sighed, although Barry could not hear it over the roar of the big diesel. He was right on the bumper of the truck full of rednecks.

"Answer me, Brenda!"

"They're part of the enforcers."

"Nice people, huh?"

He slammed into the rear of the pickup. The driver almost lost control.

"No, Barry, they are not nice people."

Again, Barry rammed the rear of the pickup. He watched as the driver grabbed for his CB mic; his own scanner light froze on 19. "Pick up my mic and hold the talk button in, Brenda. Jam the frequency."

This time, she reacted swiftly. Barry watched the driver throw his mic on the dash in disgust.

The driver of the pickup was talking frantically to the man on the right side. Barry saw the man turn and point a pistol at the rig.

Barry shifted up and rammed the pickup. The man holding the gun dropped it as his head bobbed back and forth under the impact of the Kenworth. The driver of the truck had to swing wide, and Barry closed the gap on them, pulling up alongside the truck.

"Git away from us, you crazy bassard!" the man on the right side hollered.

The driver pulled away just as Barry cut the wheel, his big bumper catching the bed of the pickup and slamming sideways. Doing at least fifty miles an hour, the pickup ran over a road sign, clobbered a mailbox, jumped the ditch, and ran headfirst into a huge tree. The tree did not move. In his mirrors, Barry saw one body that had been tossed out of the cab, lying on the ground. Another man was on the hood of the truck; he did not seem to have all of his head. The driver could not be seen. Nor would he ever see; the steering column had jammed through his chest.

Inside the house, the woman rose from bed to peer

out the curtains. "Been a terrible wreck out front, Les."

"Who is it, Mother?" the husband asked, without getting out of bed.

"It's some of those Huntley boys."

"Are they dead?"

"They appear to be."

"Good!"

"Who done this to you, Willie?" Adam asked the black man.

Willie shook his head, refusing to reply.

But they all knew.

Lucas Webster had met the group of black and white men on the road leading to Willie's home. Adam had told Lucas of his meeting with Brenda and Barry.

"You believe this Barry fellow is the government man?" Lucas had asked.

"No. But I don't believe he's who he says he is, either."

"Then . . . ?"

"I don't know, Lucas. Right now, let's get on to Willie's house. I don't like the way this night is shaping up; got a bad smell to it."

"Willie." Lucas knelt down by the old couch. "You don't have to tell us who did this—we know. It's time to make our move against Anson."

"No," Willie gasped out the word. "Not yet. I tell you who done it, but you got to promise me you won't do anythin' till I get on my feet—couple days. That's all I ask. It was Whacker and Eddie." He told them the whole disgusting story. "Some of you take Lisa

Mae to the hospital in Newburg. She's hurt bad. Shirley can't stop the bleedin'. Lisa Mae can't talk; eyes is all funny. And her stomach is all swoll up. She's hurt real bad."

Lucas nodded at two men, and they broke from the group and went into the bedroom, gently placing a quilt over Lisa, then picking the girl up.

"The doc is gonna see it was rape, Willie," Adam reminded the father. "What do you want the boys to tell him? He's gonna have to report this to Son Cody."

"That she come home thisaway, dumped on the porch, and we don't know who done it to her. It's wrong, and I know it, but this is somethin' that we've got to handle ourselves. We can't let the law proper in on this. You know how them judges is now; they'd just slap the bastards on the wrist—providin' Big Daddy Anson don't buy his boys out of it first off. It's up to us to bring justice back to Dane County. If it was ever here. Just take Lisa Mae to the hospital, that's all. Then we'll make our move."

Two men left with Shirley and the girl. "Where is Tate?" Adam asked.

"In the barn. I told him not to leave it. He won't."

"You should have gone with Lisa and Shirley, Willie," Lucas said. "Your mouth is all busted up and you don't look good."

"I'll heal," he said, but he knew he would not. He felt he had been touched by the hand of death. Knew something was very wrong inside his body. Willie wanted only a couple more days to rest. Then he would be a part of bringing justice to Dane County. In a very final way. "But it ain't time to move. Not just yet," he muttered.

"Why do you keep saying that, Willie?" Lucas asked him.

" 'Cause the feelin' ain't right. Lucas, you best lay low. You know what Hammer Kearn said. He meant it, too. No, a couple more days and the Ansons is gonna bring it to a head themselves. I really believe that. Them boys been bad before—you all know what I mean—but never like this night; never bringin' white women to let a black service them. My God, people, it was their own *sister!* That oughta tell you right there what kind of people they is. And you should have seen them boys' eyes. 'Specially Whacker. He's crazy cruel and mean; really gone around the bend. And Eddie ain't far behind him. You all know that family inbred somethin' awful. Now it's catchin' up with them."

"I still say you need to see a doctor," a man spoke.

"No. I'll heal myself. Just me and the Lord."

"Amen," Lucas said, but he wished his friend would go to the hospital. *The Lord helps those who help themselves,* he reminded himself.

"Y'all best get gone, now," Willie urged the men, " 'fore some of them Anson spies—and like I told you: they're of all colors—sees y'all. Now, get gone, boys."

Adam put a hand on Willie's head. "You're gettin' a fever, Willie. Don't wait too long 'fore you call a doc, you hear?"

Willie smiled up at him. "Yeah, I hear you, friend."

Adam returned the smile.

"People like you are in the books and the movies," Brenda said. "Not in real life. Or so I thought before this night."

They were parked in the inn's parking area. Dog was running around the complex, doing his business.

"Getting second thoughts about me, Brenda?"

"What do you think?"

"I think you should."

"Meaning?"

"Good night, Brenda."

The morning broke out of its dawning sullen, with heavy clouds hanging low in the sky, touching the higher hills of the county.

The weather-induced mood touched most of the residents of Anson, leaving them peevish and sharp-tongued.

And most of the talk in the town was about the sudden and brutal demise of Cuz's kin and the Huntley boys.

Although most were careful about how they talked on the subject—Anson had spies everywhere—most expressed absolutely no sorrow at the passing of the six rowdies who had worked for the Anson clan.

Hammer Kearn took his breakfast in the Anson mansion with Maxwell, and Maxwell laid the law down to Hammer.

"Your boys bit off more than they could chew, Hammer. And they did it on their own. I gave strict orders to leave this Barry Rivera alone. If—*if*—he was responsible for their deaths."

"He done it," Hammer spoke through clenched teeth. "Ain't no doubt in my mind about that. And I also know that him and Brenda met with Adam Wallace and that bunch of trash the same night."

"You finally succeeded in planting a man within the group?"

"No, sir. But I did have someone followin' them."

"I want no revenge on this thing, Hammer. We can't afford that luxury . . . not now. We've got to put a lid on this matter and keep that lid on the pot. It's got to die down. Do you understand me?"

"I understand, sir. I don't like it, but I do understand."

"Fine. I just hope my sons understand as well as you."

They don't, Hammer thought, but Hammer kept that to himself. "Can I speak blunt, Mister Maxwell?"

"Certainly."

"Your boys have gone pussy crazy."

"More than usual?" Maxwell asked, his tone dry.

"Yes, sir." Then he told him about what had happened at Willie Jefferson's place.

It looked to Hammer as if Maxwell Anson was going to have a stroke. He pushed his plate from him and stood up, glaring down at Hammer Kearn. "That's fact, Hammer?"

"Whacker was braggin' on it earlier this morning."

The man nodded his head. "Thank you, Hammer. Do finish your breakfast. I have some calling to do."

But as soon as Maxwell was out of sight, Hammer split. He did not want to be around when the shit hit the fan. And he knew it was going to do just that. And whoever was standing around was bound to get splattered.

Brenda was decidedly cool toward him as he walked into the office that morning. She didn't quite know what to make of a man who killed with such coldness. It's good entertainment on the TV, but in real life it was quite another story.

That was fine with Barry; he knew he should not have gotten involved with her. There was no room in his life for romance of the lasting kind. Not any more.

She settled all that quickly. "I detest what you do, Barry, but I can't help the way I feel about you as a man."

"Brenda . . ." He looked around to see if anyone might be listening. They were alone. "You have to understand that I might leave at any moment. There won't be any good-byes."

Tears came into her eyes. She quickly wiped them away. "All right."

She turned away. After a moment, she faced him.

"What are you going to do now?"

"Wait. I have a hunch it's all coming to a head—very soon. Have you heard anything about what happened over at the—what was the man's name? Jefferson?"

"Willie Jefferson. Yes." Her eyes lost some dullness, to be replaced with bright and ill-concealed anger. "Adam Wallace called me about an hour ago. He told me all about it."

"Are any of them going to the police? They have to report it. It was rape, wasn't it?"

"It was rape. Among other things. Go to the police? In Dane County? You have to be joking!"

"I can assure you, if a minor child was involved, the doctor will damn sure see that it's reported."

"Maybe to Son Cody."

"You said he was a good lawman?"

"The best."

"You want to tell me about it?"

"Let's go for a drive. There's someone I want you to meet. Lucas Webster." She smiled. "Now that I'm out of debt, I can hire someone to help out at the desk."

He returned the smile. "There you go." Taxpayer money had been used for much worse things.

"Give me five minutes. I'll meet you at your rig."

As they drove out of town, she said, "Adam told me that when he got home last night—after meeting with Willie and seeing and hearing what had happened—he sat on the edge of the bed and cried like a baby. He said that was the first time he'd cried since he was just a little boy. Then he got sick to his stomach." She told him what had transpired at the Jefferson home. And in the barn with Tate.

Barry spat out the window, trying to get rid of the sudden bad taste in his mouth. He grimaced his disgust and distaste. Animals. No, he corrected that. Not animals. That was doing a disservice to the animal kingdom. Dangerous, rabid, maddened animals was what he could compare the Anson boys to. "Makes my job much easier," he finally spoke. There was a note of finality in his statement.

And Brenda knew then that there would be a lot more blood spilled in Dane County. A lot of it spilled by this man.

What she did not know was how much blood.

Buckets full.

"Screwing a goddamned nigger!" Maxwell Anson yelled at his daughter. Ralph Causy sat by Maxwell's desk, content to let his friend and employer vent rage enough for both of them.

Personally, Ralph felt like killing his daughter.

Maxwell paced the room, pausing long enough to take several deep breaths and a long drink from a glass of water. He faced the young women. "If you oversexed, depraved bitches want a stud to service you, go into the city and hire one. Advertise in one of those filthy magazines for a man with a cock like a bull, if that's what you want. God, you both disgust me!" He shouted the words.

"The whole valley knows of your . . . your *escapade;* soon the entire county will know of it, snickering and whispering about it. Don't you sluts have any shame about you? You both must know there is a very real underground working live in this county, spying on us and reporting to . . . someone! You both must have known—surely you have that much intelligence about you—that it would go public; just like it has with every woman that fool boy has . . . has serviced. Both of you sit over there!" He pointed. "And cross your legs . . . if either of you remember how to do that."

Both young women sat down, as primly as possible. And as gently as possible.

Maxwell turned to Eddie and Whacker, and they cringed before their father even spoke a word. They were in deep shit, and both knew it. "And you two! Raping a twelve-year-old girl! My God!" He visibly and with much effort calmed himself. "Well, I've got to get you both out of the county. County! Hell, out of the country! I wish to hell I could book passage on the next space shot and send your butts to Mars; or wherever in the hell it's going.

"Sheriff Manville says the Jefferson girl might make

it. *Might* make it. But it's going to be touch and go and very, very chancy. Son Cody is just champing at the bit, just hoping she'll implicate an Anson. Even if she does live, she'll never be able to have children." He paused. "Of course, that's a blessing for taxpayers, but doesn't help solve the immediate problem. Her mind—and this is from what Sheriff Manville has been able to find out—is, well, affected. She's not going to be quite right."

"I did pop her a time or two, I reckon," Eddie confessed.

"Beating up a child," Maxwell said. "A little child. Well, I suppose this is my punishment for sins. Has to be."

Wrong. Not yet.

"I suppose God is laying His heavy hand on my shoulder for your sins."

Wrong. Wouldn't be his shoulder.

"Aw, now, Daddy—" Whacker found the nerve to say.

"Shut your mouth!"

Whacker lost his nerve.

"Hear me well," Maxwell spoke, his voice low and menacing. "I've sent word out in the county. All the notes you boys have with the white trash and niggers I'm personally recalling."

Whacker and Eddie looked as though someone had just kicked them where it hurt most.

"If you've lost money—that's your problem. But your five-for-ten loansharking is over! Finished! And from what Hammer told me, after he sent out the word, it was over as of last night. So it really doesn't make any difference. All you've done is intensify the hatred toward us all."

"Lard, Lard!" Whacker said.

"It's *Lord!*" Maxwell shouted. "Lard is something you cook with, you—you—" He could not find the words to finish.

Whacker looked astonished. "But, Daddy, 'at's what I said. Lard—lak in the Good Book!"

Maxwell suddenly had a raging headache plus an uneasy stomach. He mixed a bromide and drank it down.

Ralph said, "Where did we go wrong, Max?"

"I could write a book on where we went wrong, Ralph." He turned to once more face his two sons. He had sent word for all five to be present, but Whacker and Eddie would pass the word to them; he was certain of that. And damn soon.

"So . . . I'm sending you both away. Out to Montana for a time—a cooling-off period. Six weeks, two months. Maybe longer. I don't know. You will go to our ranch out there and you will stay in the ranch house and you will not leave the grounds. You will take your wives and your kids, and you will get the goddamn hell gone from this county! I'm having the plane serviced now. While you are out there, try screwing your wives for a change. Who knows? You might find it a novel experience. But I want you all out of this county within forty-eight hours. Do you both understand that?"

Whacker and Eddie nodded glumly. Montana? Jesus! With their *wives!* And their kids, too. What they'd done was sorta bad, they deserved a good dressing-down they reckoned . . . but this?

"Do we have to take them damn squallin' kids?" Whacker asked.

One look from his father assured him silently that

he just asked a very stupid question and he had best keep his mouth shut on the matter. And start packing.

"What about us, Daddy?" Jennifer cooed, in her best guaran-damn-teed-to-melt-the-heart-of-Daddy tone.

But this time it was all wasted. Maxwell stared her down. "I am thinking very seriously—very seriously, and I have discussed this with Ralph—of sending both of you to a convent, of sorts, in France. A very secluded and *guarded* convent. In the mountains. Once you get in, you don't get out."

"Oh, Daddy!" Jennifer laughed. "You're just a-funnin' with us!"

He stared at her. Ralph stared at Jane.

"Ain't you?" Jane asked meekly.

His look chilled them both, right down to their butts. "Would either of you care to wager on that?"

Jennifer and Jane looked at him. Looked at Ralph. Looked at each other. "No, sir!" they chimed.

Willie Jefferson shifted painfully in his bed. He felt whatever was broken inside him rear up hot and ugly at the movement. "God." He looked upward, his voice small but yet powerful in the empty house. "Give me the strength to do what I feel is right. I ain't never asked much of You, but this time I'm askin' for Your blessin' to kill a man. He's evil, Lord, through and through; don't deserve to walk Your earth. Now, I know what I'm askin' is probably wrong in the eyes of Your son, but I'm pretty much an Old Testament man. Like what You had to say about an eye for an eye and right and wrong.

"I know I'm dyin', Lord, and you know it far better

than me. Maybe it's for the best; I think it is. One thing I did that was farsighted was to keep up my GI insurance and them other policies over the years. And this property is free and clear. My Shirley is gonna be all right, and she'll have some money to look after Tate.

"Now, Tate. Don't punish him too hard, Lord. It ain't his fault the way he is. He's really a good boy at heart. It's all the evil around him. Look after him, Lord, and have mercy on all the good folks in this county, for they're many of them; but they're scared, Lord.

"Well, enough of my babblin'. Please let me live long enough to see to Whacker Anson. And if You don't see fit for me to do that . . . well, Thy will be done, then.

"Thank you, Lord."

He closed his eyes and drifted off into a light sleep, not deep enough to kill the pain that would be growing stronger and hotter within his body with each passing hour.

"A convent," Jane whispered to Jennifer. "No way, babe. There ain't no way your old man is shippin' my ass off to no nunnery in France."

"He meant it, Janey. First time I ever seen him so riled up. I just don't know what to do."

"I know one thing: we shouldn't have taken no part in rapin' that mother and her daughter."

"I don't even like to think about that. I've tried and tried to put it out of my mind. 'Bout the time I do, you got to bring it up agin."

"If Son Cody and his deputies ever find them bodies . . ."

"Aw, shit. Them bodies is nothin' but bare bones now. And that woman's husband was dropped so deep down a shaft; hell, he must have fell five or six hundred feet."

"I just ain't goin' to no convent. I just ain't gonna do it."

"Me neither."

"I ain't goin' to no damn Montanee," Eddie told his brothers. "Me and Whacker done talked it over and that's the way it's gonna be."

"We got money of our own," Whacker said. "We still got the chop shop and that brings in a right smart amount."

"Speaking of that," Slapper said, "did you git rid of that Toby feller's body?"

"Down the same shaft as that woman's husband," Eddie said.

"His rig?" Bugger asked.

"It's bein' worked on. Speakin' of rigs, I'd sure like to have that Rivera feller's rig. I'd kill that damn dog though. I hate dogs."

"Leave him alone," Banger said. "Rivera and the dog. Now look here, boys, ain't none of us ever bucked Daddy on no big decision. But they's trouble brewin' here in the county. We all heard talk this day. I think we oughta be here to he'p out. I just can't understand why he's so shook up about y'all screwin' that girl."

None of the others could, either.

Banger said, "Y'all said Willie ain't gonna press no

charges; and they's something else, too: we could always say that fool boy of his raped Jenny and Jane. They'd go along with it. Y'all say Daddy give you forty-eight hours?"

Whacker and Eddie nodded.

"Well, let's see if he'll calm down some by tomorrow. I 'spect he will."

Sheriff Jud Manville could feel the tension building in the county, and so could all his deputies. They had all reported the feeling of something growing, building. One had said the hate was so thick you could almost cut it.

Manville heaved his bulk out of the chair and paced his office. Niggers and mine trash was getting together and forming up some sort of secret organization. He'd heard rumors; didn't believe them. But now he did. Anson's iron grip on the county was slipping.

Manville pushed his beer belly in front of him and stalked out the door to his car. He'd better talk this over with Maxwell Anson. Might be bigger than either of them thought.

Several miles apart, Lucas Webster and Adam Wallace carefully cleaned their guns. About a hundred other men and women were doing the same thing in Dane County: More than a few of them had carefully looked over insurance policies and wills. More than a few felt that when it came time to make their move against the Ansons and those who supported them and that time was close, the feeling was right—there would be more than a few dead in the streets and valleys and hollows of Anson town and Dane County.

"How much further now, Colonel?"

"Not far," the tanned, hard-eyed man said. "You'll like my brother and his family. Both of you. I can't say too much for the town; don't know it that well. But it seems like a nice, peaceful little place."

Nine

"Lucas Webster," Brenda said, "I'd like you to meet Barry Rivera."

The black man laid his .30-.30 aside and rose from behind the coffee table in the small living room. He extended his hand. "Heard we had a stranger in town," he said with a smile. "Pleasure to meet you, sir. If you're a friend of Miss Brenda's, then you have to be an all-right person. We think highly of Miss Brenda."

Barry shook the callused hand. "I thank you for the trust." His eyes flicked over the old but well-cared-for lever-action rifle. "You going hunting, Mister Webster?"

"In a manner of speaking," he said, just a touch of suspicion in his voice. "Got to warn you of something, sir: if you're in sympathy with Miss Brenda's feelings toward the Anson clan, then you're going to be tarred with the same brush we've all been painted with." He grinned. "No play on words intended."

Barry grinned with him. He liked this man. "Lucas, this is none of my business, but I feel I should warn you that any type of violent vigilante action is against the law."

"You don't have to remind me, Barry. But so is rape

and murder and extortion and night riding. And a whole lot more activities those Anson boys have been and are doing. Been going on a long time, sir. And it's time the citizens did what the law won't do. Put yourself in our place."

Barry nodded. He knew the feeling. He looked at Brenda. "Now maybe you'll tell me why you wanted me to meet Lucas?"

"So you could perhaps talk some sense into his head. Maybe keep Lucas and a whole lot of other good men from getting killed or put in prison."

"Including yourself, Brenda?" Barry smiled at her.

"I don't know what you mean!"

"You were with me last night. That makes you a part of it. You want to turn me in for what I did to those rednecks?"

"I'm missing something here," Lucas said.

"I was attacked last evening. Brenda and I. I don't believe in running if one has the wherewithal to defend oneself."

"Those trashy Huntley boys?" the minister asked.

"I believe that was one of the names mentioned."

Lucas shrugged. "A half of dozen less rednecks in the world."

"Lucas!" Brenda said. "I can't believe you said that."

"Miss Brenda, the time for talking is past. We're going to make our move. I would suggest you stay low."

Brenda stared at him. "But you've always been the most peaceful man I ever knew!"

"Peaceful men sometimes have to fight, child. When all else fails, it's time to fight." He looked at Barry. "You're a fighting man, aren't you, sir?"

"I have been known to ball a fist every now and then, yes, sir."

"And you still maintain that you are not the government man that is rumored to be in Dane County?"

"Lucas, if I were that government man, would I be taking part in something illegal?"

Lucas threw back his head and laughed. "Oh, that's funny, Barry. Heavens! A government man doing something illegal? That's unthinkable!"

That went right by Brenda's head. "Lucas, where is your wife?"

"I sent her off to visit her sister in Louisville. I wanted her just as far away from Dane County as possible."

Brenda sighed and shook her head. "A person reads about something like this happening. But it's always in some far-off place, never in your own hometown."

Barry stood silent until Lucas said, "I really don't think you're what you say you are, but Brenda trusts you. You want in on our little upcoming battle?"

Barry shook his head. "I'm not going to sideline the issue, Lucas. But when I make a move, if I do, it will be as a loner. I do understand why you men are preparing to fight. Should have been done a long time ago."

Lucas nodded his agreement. "Adam still figures you're here to do more than take pictures."

"Could be."

"I wouldn't want you to get hurt, Barry; don't you and Miss Brenda get all caught up in the tide when it comes roaring in."

"I can assure you, Lucas, I will do my best to keep both of us clear."

The men stood looking at each other until Lucas

said, "How come I get the feeling that you're ex-military?"

"Aren't we all?"

The minister's eyes were cool and knowing. "Some more than others."

"You think it's really coming to a head?" Maxwell asked the sheriff.

"Yes, sir. I surely do think that. All my men report the same thing: a feelin' of open hatred and hostility. After them Huntley boys was killed? That old couple out there didn't even report the wreck. Told me it would have given them a great deal of pleasure to see the buzzards eat them ol' boys. That's strong talk, Mister Anson."

"They actually said that?"

"Both of them."

"That's callous, Jud."

"That's how much we're hated, Mister Anson."

"I should have seen it coming. But I handed out food baskets at Thanksgiving and Christmas. I built and staffed a hospital. What else do these trash want?"

"I know you been a good man, Mister Anson. But it's too quiet around the county. Men stayin' home from work. Sendin' their wives and kids out of the county. It's boilin' strong, now; lid's about to blow slap off."

"We're going to have to play our cards close to the vest, Jud."

"Yes, sir. And when we move, there can't be no bluffin' this time."

"I spent ten thousand dollars for a company picnic last Fourth. Ungrateful bastards and bitches." He sighed heavily. "I was going to send Whacker and Eddie out of the county. Now . . . I just don't know."

"They both commissioned deputies. I could shore use 'em if this thing pops—and it's goin' to. We gonna need all the manpower we can get."

"All right, Jud. All right. I'll call the boys in and tell them. All my boys carry badges, don't they?"

"Yes, sir."

"Do they know anything at all about the workings of the law, Jud?"

"Not a goddamn thing."

That's understandable, Maxwell thought. "Get hold of Tay Blessing. We'll need him to stay close. Do you have any firm ideas as to just who is fronting this group of . . . malcontents?"

"Pretty good idea. Nothing solid though. Everything points to Adam Wallace and Lucas Webster."

"Disgusting! A white man teaming up with a nigger. This country is going to hell in a slop jar, Jud."

"Yes, sir. Shore is."

"The followers of these . . . people?"

"Well, sir"—Jud scratched his half-bald head—"we know 'bout ten or twelve of them for shore. But they's near-bouts a hundred, so I'm told."

Maxwell whirled around, staring at the man. "What did you say, Jud?" He wore a startled look on his face. "Did you say a hundred?"

"Yes, sir," the sheriff replied glumly. "At least that. My guess would be twenty-five or thirty more than that. County's sold out of ammo. Ellen County, too. Sheriff Cody, so I'm told, is gettin' some sort of grim satisfaction out of all the rumors. If they are rumors," he added unhappily.

"We could ask for the National Guard," Maxwell suggested. "Or the State Police."

"Have to notify the governor with either one of them thoughts, Mister Maxwell. And he'd probably suggest we ask Sheriff Cody for help."

"You're right. And wouldn't Son just love that." Maxwell brushed back a lock of silver-gray hair from his forehead. "That sanctimonious bastard!"

Sheriff Manville braced himself for the outburst he knew was surely coming from Maxwell Anson.

Maxwell Anson and Son Cody had hated one another for years. Maxwell because Sheriff Cody could not and would not be bought off—for any price—and ran a fair and honest department. Son because he felt—and rightly so—the entire Anson clan and followers were nothing but white trash, troublemakers, thugs, and spoiled whores. And arrogant assholes, to boot. He was right on all counts. Therefore, no Anson attempted to throw his or her weight around in Ellen County; indeed, they exercised the utmost caution to carefully avoid Son Cody's county and his straight-arrow deputies. The chief deputy, one James Willard, had the honor and privilege of hammering Bugger's head one night with a nightstick.

Bugger had bragged that no gawdamn skinny-assed deputy sheriff was gonna put him in the bucket.

He hadn't gone to jail. He had gone to the hospital . . . then to jail.

Son Cody had also arrested Jennifer for indecent behavior with a juvenile. But those charges were finally dropped when the juvenile found himself the proud owner of a new Corvette. But his joy was short-lived; every time he turned around there was an Ellen

County deputy writing him a ticket for one thing or the other.

It was not wise to cross Son Cody.

Sheriff Jud Manville waited until Maxwell ran down in his damning and cursing of Son Cody, took a deep breath, and began counting on his fingers. "Them we strongly suspect of being a part of the group agin you is Johnny Springer, Lucas Webster, Adam Wallace, Henry Castine, James Hart, Robert Washington, Paul Noonen, Lee Wyatt, Van McBride, Goldie Harris, Bill Watson—"

Maxwell waved him silent; a curt, impatient slash of the hand. "Enough, Jud! I don't care to hear the names of every white trash and nigger in the county." He was silent for a moment, his lips pursed and his brow wrinkled in thought. "All right, Jud. I think we made a mistake by not taking this matter seriously from the outset; we could have and should have crushed it before it ever got fully organized. Now it seems it's too late for any easy solution. When you get back to your office, get on the phone and start pulling men in. Deputize them—*all* of them. I want this as legal as possible if, or when, any shooting starts."

"Yes, sir."

"If one of those men you mentioned, or any you think is involved in this . . . uprising against us even spits on the sidewalk, I want him, or her, arrested. You can get your men to start planting some dope in homes and vehicles around the county. You have a drawer full of signed search warrants by the judge, don't you?"

"Yes, sir."

"Fill in the date and start breaking down doors. We can fill the jail with suspected pushers and ushers;

keep them long enough to break the back of this revolt before it gets started full steam."

Sheriff Manville smiled. He liked that idea. It wasn't against any law and did not violate any constitutional rights to strip-search people before they were put in a cell. He'd even had his own finger—illegally—up the snatch of more than one fine-looking gal thataway; liked it even better when he could put on the rubber gloves and stick them in the ass. Like to hear them cry and beg in embarrassment. But most of the time he used Erin for the women. She liked that. And Bugger Anson had earned his nickname more than once with a male troublemaker. Kinda took all the fight and spirit to have Bugger take them thataway. Plumb humiliating. Painful too. And Bugger liked to do it. He wouldn't want to tell Maxwell, but Bugger was slap-dab nuts. And the others wasn't that far behind him. No . . . Bugger wasn't nuts neither, the sheriff revised his opinion. They was all just cruel mean.

Maxwell said, "Most of those you named owe me money at the bank. I can get my loan officers to start putting pressure on them; enough to get them to back off—" Noticing Jud shaking his head, a hound-dog look on his fat face, he stopped. "Why are you shaking your head, Jud?"

"They ain't gonna back off this time, Mister Maxwell. No matter what you do. We might choke it down some, but that's all. They're gonna take this fight to the bitter, bloody end. Believe me. You 'member readin' about all that trouble down in Tennessee 'bout '46–'47? All the veterans got riled up over some rigged election, I believe it was?"

"Yes. It was over an election. So what about it, Jud?"

"Well, this is gonna be a lot worse. I believe it's gonna be killin' bad, sir. I really believe that, sir."

Maxwell could but shake his head. "How did it get this bad without my knowing it?"

"Mister Maxwell . . . I . . . ain't real certain how to say this. But, well, them boys of your'n . . ."

"I know, Jud. Believe me, I know. I don't want to hear about them. You wouldn't be able to say anything I don't already know. I don't think you could, that is. But rehashing won't solve a thing; all that is water under the bridge. Tell me the truth, Jud. As a father, if yours had behaved as badly as mine—and I admit they've been rowdy—would you have let one of them go to prison?"

The sheriff did not hesitate. "No, sir. Not if I could have prevented it." He paused, then plunged ahead. "But I damn shore would have cut me a limb from a piss elm tree and plumb wore me some asses out with it."

Maxwell smiled, then chuckled. "Yes. I certainly failed there. Hell, I failed in many ways. I admit it."

"Yes, sir. All right, sir. I'll tell the Kearn boys to gear up for trouble, and I'll tell Hammer to come here to the mansion, armed."

"You think that is necessary?"

"Yes, sir, I sure do. I surely think we are goin' to have us a bloodbath in Dane County, and for the life of me, I can't figure one damned way to prevent it from happenin'. And Mister Maxwell . . . ?"

"I know," the man said. "When it does, after it's all over, we're going to have federal people crawling on top of each other getting in here. And those fucking press people will be all over us like maggots on the dead."

"Yes, sir."

A servant stuck her head into the study. "I'm very sorry to have to bother you, Mister Anson. But there has been some trouble out at your airport, sir."

"What kind of trouble?"

"Your planes have been tampered with, both of them, sir."

Maxwell felt something cold and oozy slide about in his stomach, the feeling not unlike a sackful of leeches slowly crawling about. "How were they tampered with?"

"The mechanic and pilot said they were warming up the planes today when both engines quit on your Beechcraft. Somebody jimmied the oil lines and rigged the gauges to show normal. The engines are ruined. Then they went to the big plane and found it had been shot all to pieces; said it looked like someone laid back a-ways and used it for target practice. They said it was a real mess; some of the bullets smashed up the panel. Be days or weeks in fixing them both."

Maxwell silently cursed for a moment. "Very well. Thank you, Mrs. Croffton."

"Sir."

She waited until she had closed the door before letting her smile surface. Her sons had done a real good job on the planes. She was proud of them both. The Ansons were evil people, and she'd be happy to see them all get their comeuppance. The sooner the better.

Sheriff Manville looked at the patriarch of the Anson family. "We better get ready, Mister Maxwell," he said very softly.

"Yes." Maxwell nodded his head. "Get the boys."

"Your boys?"

The shake of the head was minute. "No. You know the boys I'm talking about, Jud. And get rid of that goddamned Lucas Webster. Tell Hammer to forget about coming over here. I can look after myself. Tell him to take care of Lucas Webster—finish it!"

"Yes, sir."

"Can you shoot?" Barry asked Brenda.

She nodded her head. "Not very well. Oh, I suppose I could hit a person if he wasn't standing too far from me—with a pistol, that is." She looked at him, serious eyes on his face. "Barry, shouldn't we be doing something to prevent what we know is going to happen?"

"What would you suggest?" He already knew what she might say.

"Call in the state police or the National Guard, maybe?"

"The state police and Guard will probably be in after it's all over. Even if you did call them, all you have to offer them is rumors. Nothing has happened that they don't already know about—and you can bet on that."

"You think they have some sort of . . . well, undercover person in here now?"

"It wouldn't surprise me. And no"—he smiled—"it isn't me."

"I wouldn't bet on anything right now."

Barry looked at his watch. "Does Newberg have a nice kennel?"

"Oh, yes. Big place with a large exercise yard. Why?"

"Come on. Let's go for a drive."

* * *

Dog didn't like it, but he didn't kick up too much of a fuss. Especially when a young lady started petting and cooing and oohing over him. She assured Barry that Dog would be well taken care of; she might even take him home, if Barry didn't mind.

Barry didn't mind.

On the way back to Anson, Brenda said, "You care for your dog but don't give a damn for many people. You're a strange man, Barry."

"I like animals; I always have. They are a hell of a lot more loyal and loving than many people." They were approaching the intersection that would take them to town. "Do you know where Johnny South lives, Brenda?"

"Sure. Just outside of town, east, on County Fourteen. Why?"

"Point the way"

She gave him directions while Barry kept an eye on his mirrors. A pickup truck had appeared, hanging back, but staying with them.

"You know that truck, Brenda?"

She glanced in her side mirror. "Erin Ramsey. She's one of the Anson loyalists. I was wondering when she'd make an appearance."

"Why do you say that?"

"She's Banger and Bugger's favorite person; just as sick and evil and perverted as any of them. I'm very surprised she wasn't a part of the rape and murder of that family."

"Maybe she was."

"If she was, we'll probably never know."

"Why do you say that?"

"If shooting starts, Erin is sure to be one somebody will shoot. She's pure filth."

"We'll drive past Johnny's house; well past it, and pull over to the side of the road. I want a look at this Erin person."

As they passed Johnny's small house, Brenda said, without turning her head. "That's his house. He's home. That's his pickup in the drive."

"And that's him on the porch." Barry looked at the man sitting in a chair. Same ol' Puff; didn't look like he'd changed in fifteen years—from what he could tell at this distance. And Barry was very curious as to why Puff was in the county. Who had sent him? Or who in the county, perhaps, had sent *for* him?

He dismissed the last thought. Puff was solid Agency. Took orders only from them.

"You have a puzzled look on your face, Barry."

"Johnny. I just can't make his connection in the county."

"So that's two of us who are puzzled."

Barry looked at her.

"I don't know what you're doing in the county, either."

Barry drove about a mile up the road, until he came to an old falling-down barn. He pulled over, pretending to stare at the structure, or what was left of it. The pickup drove slowly by. Barry looked at the woman behind the wheel. She was a small, dark-haired woman, with a very deep tan. Her face was savage looking.

She turned her head, and for a moment, their eyes were locked.

"Hideous looking," Brenda said. "She gives me the

creeps. She could have very well been a guard at a Nazi concentration camp."

Barry agreed with that. "Where is this so-called chop shop?"

"About ten miles further on."

"Let's go see it."

"Are you crazy!"

"No," Barry said, putting the truck into gear. "I just don't have any restrictions on me, that's all."

Brenda didn't have to ask what he meant by that. She knew. Now.

Ten

Granger Kildare put his hand on the phone, thought for a moment, then slowly removed his fingers from the receiver without ever taking it from the cradle. He was in a mental quandary. He knew from a gut feeling that Dane County, especially the town of Anson, was about to blow wide open, but he didn't have any hard evidence to report to his chief in Louisville.

He just knew it was.

He knew where the chop shop was, and had the authority to go in and bust it wide open. But that was small potatoes. That could wait until later.

Special Agent Granger Kildare, of the Federal Bureau of Investigation, knew how to trust his gut instincts. He was Kentucky born and reared, just north of Paintsville, on the Levisa Fork. Granger had seen things turn violent in a hurry when coal miners and mountain folk got pissed off and decided to take justice into their own work-hardened hands.

The results of that were, more often than not, very bloody.

And Granger knew that was just hours, perhaps minutes, away from happening right there in Dane County. Knew it, but couldn't prove it.

Granger knew he had enough hard evidence to arrest Ralph Causy, and maybe a federal judge would sign a warrant for the arrest of Maxwell Anson on a number of small charges—but damn it, it just wasn't enough to put the bastards away for any length of time. The appeals would, he knew, run on for years and years.

And the victims of Maxwell's sons' perversion just would not, by God, take their grievances into a court of law.

Granger understood. He didn't like it, but he understood the people's reluctance.

Granger knew, but couldn't prove, that mine inspectors were being bought off; knew the chiefs of police in the county and the sheriff and the patrolmen and deputies, and the mayor—hell, everybody that was somebody—were in Maxwell Anson's pocket. Knew it, but just couldn't prove it so that it would hold up in court.

"Shit!" the FBI man said.

Men loyal to Maxwell Anson began gathering slowly at Anson Hall—the town's so-called civic center, located just on the outskirts of town. The men were being called in from all over the county. They were a trashy, mean-eyed bunch, all owing something to the Ansons. They were mine foremen and coal haulers and supervisors and mechanics and roughnecks—all receiving money, in one way or another, from one Anson or another. They all carried duffle bags containing sidearms and billy clubs. A long table in the hall had been loaded with rifles and shotguns.

Another table contained a huge coffee urn and sandwiches.

Sheriff Jud Manville waited in the hall, beside a box of badges. When the men had fixed their coffee and picked up sandwiches, taken their seats and settled down, then Jud explained the situation to them and what, exactly, would be required of them.

The men smiled as they fingered the badges, then raised their hands to take the oath. They liked this method of doing things even better than just plain-ol' bustin'-heads type of work. This here was legal. They liked that. They'd been busting heads and kicking ass of union organizers and sympathizers for years, whipping (literally) into line any Anson employee who dared question the work practices, pay habits, or working conditions of the Anson empire.

But this was gonna be fun. Nothing like a good rough-and-tumble fight to get the blood stirring in a man. A real man. Especially when you knew you weren't going to jail if you accidentally killed somebody.

They all knew, to a man, that this here mess wouldn't take too long to straighten out. They all knew they was tough and bad.

Just ask their wives and girlfriends; the men had slapped them around enough. And their kids. Yes, indeed, rough and tough.

"Y'all stay loose as a goose and ready to move at a moment's notice, hear?" Sheriff Manville told the gathering of rough and tough and ready men. "Might not need you boys, but a man don't never know what the malcontents"—Jud remembered that word from his conversations with Maxwell Anson; sounded right impressive—"might git in their heads to do. Got cots and blankets here in the hall." Manville smiled, and looked like a hog at the trough. "Erin and some of her friends is comin' over di-rectly." A loud cheer went up at that news. "So's you boys won't git lonesome tonight. For now, y'all jist stay ready and wait for word to move."

Manville started to step down from the podium, then paused, looking around at the large group of men. He said, "Y'all get them rifles and shotguns over yonder on the table and get 'em oiled up and loaded. I got me a hunch you're gonna need 'em."

"Barry!" Brenda said, a note of desperation in her voice. "Nobody goes in there. Do you have a death wish?"

Barry glanced in his mirrors. It was as he suspected. Johnny's pickup truck was pulling in behind the Kenworth. "Stay in the rig," Barry told her.

She did, but lowered the windows so she could listen.

"Puff," Barry said.

"Captain. Been a few years."

"Too many." Barry smiled at the M-10 slung over Puff's shoulder. "You expecting trouble, Puff?"

"A man never knows. I hear talk that you're a one-man wrecking crew, Dog."

"Hell, Puff, you've been that for years!"

The two men shared a laugh.

"I won't ask you questions, Puff; you don't ask me any."

"That's a deal." He looked toward the huge metal building. "Folks inside that building have caused a lot of grief to a lot of good people."

"Is that right?"

"Yeah. You know what really pissed me off, Dog?"

Barry waited.

"A lot of drivers carry dogs with them for company."

"Yeah. I do, too."

"Those in that chop shop, they bring a rig in to strip it down for parts. Sometimes the driver they stole it from has him a little pet riding with him."

Barry knew what was coming next.

"Those rednecks in there, they just shoot the dog. Just shoot it. Man that would do that to a little animal is lower than baboon shit as far as I'm concerned."

Barry started laughing softly. Puff hadn't been sent in here; he'd come on his own. Puff hadn't gotten all pissed off about human rights; he'd gotten all bent out of shape about animals' rights!

"I just can't stand to see an animal abused. Tears me up somcthing awful. I'm getting mad just standing here thinking about it."

Barry blurted out, "But you're in the computer. Central told me that much."

"What the government don't know won't hurt them. I'm on vacation."

"Well, let's go have some fun then."

"Sounds good to me. Dog, there are no innocent men in there. I checked it. They're all party to murder and rape and torture and just about anything else you'd care to name. I don't leave witnesses."

"I've never found it to be a good habit, myself."

A man stepped out of the huge building. He shouted, "What the hell do you men think you're doing out there?"

"Damned unfriendly bastard, isn't he?" Puff commented.

"Not at all overflowing with the milk of human kindness, I will have to say."

"Git your goddamn asses outta here!" the man shouted.

Puff looked at the massive bumper of the Kenworth. "I have never seen a bumper quite like that. That isn't a truck; that's a damned tank!"

"Goddammit!" the man shouted. "Do you men hear me? I said clear the hell out of here 'fore we'uns decide to whup your asses."

"I think he flunked grammar," Barry said.

"He's about to flunk life," Puff said, looking at the windows. "Bulletproof?"

"So I've been told."

"Armor plate, too?"

"That's what they told me."

"I bet that thing could ram right through that tin building."

"Let's do it, then."

They climbed in, sending Brenda to the sleeper with orders to hang on. Her eyes were wide and she was scared.

"You want to stay out here in Puff's pickup?" Barry asked her.

She shook her head.

"Then hang on!"

"That's better!" the man hollered. "I knowed you'd turn yeller and run."

"Isn't he going to be the surprised one?" Puff said, grinning.

Barry checked his M-10, sticking full clips behind his belt.

"You got any portable bang-bangs?" Puff asked.

"Sackful of grenades in the sleeper. Brenda, open that compartment there and hand me that sack. That's it. Thank you."

"You're welcome," she said automatically. "What in the hell are you men going to do?"

"Probably make a disgusting mess," Puff told her. "Regrettably unavoidable, however."

"Quite," Barry added.

"You guys are crazy!" She summed it up.

"Hey!" the man hollered. "Move on out, you assholes."

"Shall we move on out, my good man?" Puff said with a smile.

"We shall do so smartly," Barry replied, dropping the Kenworth into gear. "Hang on, Brenda!"

Brenda started praying softly.

Barry rammed through the chain-link gates and rumbled and snorted and rolled toward the man standing in front of the building housing the chop shop.

"Hey!" he hollered. "Hol' up! Crazy bassards!"

Another man ran out the door, a shotgun in his hands. He pointed it at the charging Kenworth with the massive steel bumper. Puff leaned out and leveled his Mac-10. Lead started humming and howling and bouncing and flying. The man with the shotgun doubled over and sat down as the line of lead stitched him across the belly. The shotgun went off on impact with the ground, the charge striking the first guard in the head.

The man went down, half of his face missing.

"Hit the floor, Brenda," Barry shouted. "And hang on!" She hit the floor just as the Kenworth rammed through the tin building, sending bits of metal and tools and insulation flying in all directions from the impact.

Barry saw Toby's rig parked in the center of the large building. Someone had just started stripping the tractor.

A slug ricocheted off the cab as a dozen men appeared, all of them carrying weapons.

Leveling his own Mac, Barry held the trigger back and cleared one line of charging men, the slugs spinning them and dropping them to the oily concrete floor, in various degrees of pain and injury and death.

Puff spotted a man running for a wall phone. Puff sent the man face first to the floor with a line of 9mm holes smoking on and in his back.

Barry pulled the pin on a grenade and chucked it over the cab of a pickup truck, where he'd seen several men run. The frag grenade blew, blowing parts of human bodies up and over and onto the truck and splattering other vehicles and the wall with gore.

"Good show, my boy!" Puff yelled over the rolling racket of gunfire and smoke and yelling and screaming and confusion.

"Thank you," Barry replied modestly.

"About four guys behind that pickup truck right over there!" Puff pointed. "And I do so hate to waste precious ammo. Do you get my—ah, smashing point?"

Barry laughed and clutched down, floorboarding the pedal. The massive nose and steel bumper hit the pickup, practically picking it up and slamming it and the men behind it against a forklift. He dropped the Kenworth into reverse as the men were screaming their way into Hell.

A bullet sent bits of paint and metal into Barry's

cheek, bringing blood to the surface. He shifted up and pointed the nose of the tractor at the man who had been so rude as to shoot at him. Screaming his fright, the man dropped his pistol and tried to run away from the monster bearing down on him, belching clouds of smoke.

He ran into a small wood-and-glass office. Barry drove the office, the man, and a second man who had been hiding in the office straight through the wall of the chop shop, grinding them under the massive tires of the truck.

Spinning the wheel, Barry again entered the building, through the original hole he'd punched.

Two men were trying to force open a back door that had obviously buckled and jammed from the building's being slammed into. Puff ended their efforts abruptly.

The place began to be as quiet as a tomb; which it had suddenly become for about a dozen men.

He looked back at Brenda. She had fainted. Just to make sure, Barry checked her pulse: strong and steady.

Grinning at Puff, he climbed down, followed by Puff, and began inspecting the rubble. Barry had an idea about the wounded men. He told Puff and the man grinned.

"I love it! Let's look for records."

"You look. I want to look inside Toby's Peterbilt.

He found a bloody shirt and a bloody cowboy hat. He recognized the hat as the one Toby had been wearing back at the truck stop.

"Bastards!" he cursed.

He found a wounded man and slapped him to consciousness. "FBI!" Barry snarled at him. He pointed toward Puff. "That's Jennings from Treasury. You're in deep shit, boy, you know that?"

"I'll tell ever'thang I knows! Man, ya'll don't play far, atall."

"You tell it to Son Cody."

"Son Cody! Man, I'd rather tell hit to the devil his-salf!"

Barry leveled his Mac and the man pissed on him-self.

"I'll be more'n happy to talk to Son, I swear hit!"

Puff produced a set of handcuffs, and Barry hand-cuffed the slightly wounded man to the roll bar of a stripped-down hot rod.

"Ah can't git a-loose!" the man squalled. "Hale's faire, hit'll take me hours to get to Ellen County all strung up lak 'is!"

"You'll make it by about midnight," Puff told him. Then dumped several bodies into the back of the rod.

"Oh, Lard, Lard!" the man hollered.' "At ain't de-cent, man!"

"You have the gall to talk about decency?" Barry asked. He looked at the man's driver's license. "I'll just keep this. Turn it over to the IRS."

"Why for would you do somethang awful lak 'at? Man, ain't I in 'nuff trouble?"

"That's just in case you don't make it to Son Cody right at midnight."

"I'm gonna make hit! I promise! Whut's so special 'bout midnight?"

"He'll be waiting for you at the jail at that time. Now clear on out of here!"

"I can't shift and drive with no one hand!"

Puff placed the muzzle of his Mac against the man's head.

"Yeah, I reckon I can do 'er, too. You just watch me, boys."

He bucked and stalled and roared and ground the gears, but he was giving it his all as he topped the hill and was out of sight.

"You suppose he'll really go to Son Cody?" Puff asked.

Barry laughed. "I don't know. It's worth a try, though. Let's get the hell out of here!"

"Dog?"

"Hey?"

"We probably won't see each other again on this operation. You take care."

"Keep your head down, Puff."

"Same to you."

In the truck, Brenda was up, albeit looking a little green around the mouth from the sights and smells of recent combat.

"Why is he called Puff?" she asked.

"Listen."

The faint sounds of whistling reached them. Johnny, whistling "Puff, the Magic Dragon."

Eleven

A light rain slicked the streets and the highways, and glistening wet diamonds formed momentarily on leaves and branches before sliding and falling gently to the ground.

The townspeople who played neither side of the street in the Anson ball game, trying to walk a middle road and to remain as inconspicuous as possible, seemed to sense trouble was just around the corner. They closed their shops and stores and went home, locking the doors, remaining inside.

The streets of Anson became deserted; not even a dog or cat could be seen. Anson became so unusually quiet for so early on a Saturday evening that Brenda had dismissed the kitchen help and the waitresses and closed the dining area. She sat with Barry in the small private dining area, over coffee.

"What happens if someone like you gets out of control, Barry?"

"Assuming I know what you're talking about, and I have to assume this is only hypothetical, I should imagine we'd be destroyed."

She nodded her head. "More coffee?"

"Thank you."

"My, aren't we being polite this evening." It was not

a question, and the sarcasm was thick as honey in her mouth.

"Please remember that I told you your feelings toward me would change as time went along."

"I get all the luck," she said bitterly. "I meet a man that I truly like, and he turns out to be a real-life Dirty Harry."

Barry grinned. "It's a tough job, baby, but somebody has to do it."

"Please spare me that crap!" She looked into his eyes. "Suppose you wanted to quit, get out, retire . . . could you?"

Barry thought about that for a moment. "I don't know. I doubt it. Hell, Brenda, I just don't know if I could or not."

"Of course, this is all hypothetical."

"Certainly."

She said a very ugly word.

"But you're doing what you want to do?" she asked.

Again, Barry pondered that question. "Yes, Brenda. Yes, I am. And I don't think I have to explain that to you. I believe you understand."

She shuddered. "God forgive me, but I do understand." She looked up when a light tapping sounded on the dining room door. Adam Wallace stood there, hat in hand. She invited him in and poured coffee. The miner looked suspiciously at Barry.

"He's on our side, Adam," she told him. "Believe me, I know that for a rock-solid fact." The memories of that afternoon at the chop shop were etched forever in her brain.

The two men sat and stared at each other.

"Yeah," Adam finally spoke. "Yeah, I reckon he is. Somebody played hell out at an Anson-owned garage today. Dead bodies all over the damn place. Sheriff Manville is jumpin' hot. Some of his kin was runnin' that chop shop."

"I'm so sorry to hear that," Barry said.

"Yeah? I can see you're all tore up about it."

"Any warrants out on whatever it was happened?" Barry asked.

"Nope." The young miner looked at Barry, then shifted his gaze to Brenda. He stared down at his coffee cup. "Sheriff Manville's deputized all the Anson boys. He's pulled in all the strikebreakers from around the county. Fifty-sixty of them. At least that many. They're all armed and primed and cocked for trouble. Down to the Hall. Looks like it's all gonna blow this night. We've agreed that we're all goin' through the wire this time around. No backin' up."

"I suppose it's time," Brenda said. "No chance that it will blow over?"

"No," Adam dismissed that. "But there's more I ain't told y'all. Lucas Webster is gone—disappeared. Can't find him no place. They've arrested Goldie Harris; took him to jail. They roughed him up pretty bad while they was doin' it, too. He was bleedin' when they chunked him into the cage in the car. No tellin' what they'll do to him once they get him into jail. Place is like a fort."

"What do you mean, Adam?" Brenda asked. "About what they'll do to him?"

"You wouldn't know about that place, Miss Brenda. But those of us who walk on the other side of your place in society do. They've been some awful things done to people in that jail. Rape, torture—things I wouldn't feel right discussin' in your presence."

"Drug searches?" Barry asked.

"Oh, yeah. On both men and women. My sister was one of them that Sheriff Manville personally searched." He frowned. "It wasn't very nice. Worse yet when Erin got to messin' with her."

Brenda looked from man to man. "I don't understand any of this!"

"Maybe your man will explain it to you after I'm gone, Miss Brenda. I damn sure don't intend to talk no more about it."

Brenda accepted that. "What do you think is happening to Goldie?"

"Oh, yeah," Slapper said, standing over the young white man lying on the concrete cell floor. "Yeah, Goldie, yeah, you will. I'll make you a bet on that, buddy."

The man shook his head and smiled grimly. "No way, Slapper." Blood dripped from his mouth; a dark bruise was deepening on the side of his jaw. His mouth was puffy where he'd been hit.

"What you tryin' to get him to do, Slapper?" a deputy asked.

"Bark lak a dawg, 'at's all."

"Hell, get one of them new cattle prods outta my truck, Slapper," he suggested with a nasty grin. "They brand-new models; really got some juice to 'em. Touch it agin his nuts and hit the juice. I guaran-damn-tee you he'll be more 'n happy to bark and howl and sniff assholes with the bes' hound in the county. 'At'd be fun to watch."

Goldie lay on the floor and remained silent. He had a hunch this was going to be a long, long night for him. He just hoped he'd survive it.

Slapper grinned. "Oh, yeah! Now, that air's a right good idea, Jerry. You go on and git me one of them prods." He turned back to Goldie as the deputy left the basement cell area.

"We gonna have us some fun, Goldie."

"Fuck you!" Goldie told him.

Slapper grinned. "You ain't near'bouts gonna be so tough in a minute, boy."

"What's goin' on down here?" Sheriff Jud Manville's voice echoed around the concrete and steel passageway

"Aw, hell, Jud," Slapper said. "We wasn't gonna hurt him much. Just tickle his balls with a cattle prod, is all. You know this damn Goldie's been agitatin' around here for years. Stirrin' up trouble for all of us. 'Sides, hit'll be his word agin ours. Ain't 'at right?"

Sheriff Manville looked at one of his deputies. "Where's that damn Kildare? I ain't never trusted him too much."

"Aw, he's all right, Sheriff," the deputy replied. "He's just on the quiet side, is all. He ain't around; on patrol."

"I never did lak him," Slapper said.

"He's a nigger lover," yet another deputy said. "And he thinks he's better than us 'uns."

Manville brushed all that aside and stepped into the cell housing Goldie. He glared down at the man. "All right, Goldie, here it is. Listen good, boy. You gimme the names and when all this crap is gonna start, and where, and you can walk out of here a free man. No marks, no more cuts and bruises, and no gittin' hit with a cattle prod to the balls. How about it, Goldie? You help us, and we'll help you."

Goldie knew he was gonna get the shit beat out of

him no matter which way he went. Slapper had hated him ever since that night Goldie had knocked him on his fat ass in front of witnesses. He grinned up at Sheriff Manville. "Names, huh?"

"That's right, Goldie."

"OK." The man's grin widened. "Sure."

"Git him up on his feet, boys," Manville ordered. "Start flappin' that mouth, Goldie."

Goldie smiled and said, "George Washington, Thomas Jefferson, Abe Lincoln, John L. Lewis, Harry Truman, Elvis . . ."

Manville flushed angrily and drove the end of the nightstick into Goldie's stomach, slamming the wind from him. Goldie doubled over, the blow knocking him to his knees. Manville brought his knee up hard, savagely, onto the man's nose, the nose crunching under the impact. Goldie screamed as the blood spurted, staining his shirtfront.

"No-good, smart-mouthed white trash!" Manville panted the words.

Through his pain, Goldie managed a laugh. "You call me trash? That's a joke, Manville."

"Here you go, Sheriff." Jerry handed him the cattle prod.

Manville smiled as he gripped the rubber handle of the long, voltage-charged cattle prod. "This here is one of them new jobs, ain't it?"

"Yes, sir!"

"Thing all juiced up good?"

"Yes, sir. That there prod—on full charge—will knock a dog to its knees. I done it just for fun lots of times. I got that one set on half-charge."

"Oh, yeah?" Manville smiled. "Do tell. Jerk them jeans off, Goldie."

Goldie didn't fight it; no point in getting hurt worse than he had to. He was naked from the waist down, cold on the bare floor.

Manville's eyes were evil. "Your wife's name is Sue, ain't it, Goldie?"

"Leave my wife out of this," he gasped, then spat blood and a broken tooth onto the cell floor. "She hasn't done nothin' to nobody."

"Aw, now, Goldie," Manville teased, grinning at the man's efforts to cover his nakedness. "You ought'n to feel thataway. Tell me something: your wife got pretty good pussy; move her ass good?"

Goldie looked up at the man, hate in his eyes. "You goddamn low-life son of a bitch!"

Manville touched the back of Goldie's hand with the prod. Goldie screamed and jerked as the battery voltage lanced through him.

"When you talk to me, boy!" Manville shouted, his voice bouncing around the cell area, "you say: 'Yes, sir, Sheriff Manville.' You got all that, you trouble-makin' bastard?"

Goldie glared up at him. "I'm tellin' you now, Sheriff. It's all comin' down on your head, real soon."

"Well, now!" Manville drew back. "Hell, I per-ceeve that as a dire threat to my life. I can't tolerate that." He shoved the tip of the prod between Goldie's legs and hit the switch.

Goldie screamed in pain as the prod touched his testicles.

"I asked you a question, trash. Now what you got to say?"

"Yes, sir, Sheriff Manville." Goldie managed to gasp out the words.

"That's better, boy. Now then, I asked you how your wife was in bed, didn't I?"

Goldie put his head on the concrete and wept.

"You know, Sheriff," a deputy said. "That's a right good idea."

Manville looked at him. "What do you mean by that?"

"Sue Harris is a fine-lookin' head. Don't you reckon she'd be right obligin' to some of us if we was to spare her man any more hurt? How 'bout it, Sheriff?"

Manville thought on that. He'd done it before. Couldn't see no harm in it. They wasn't nothin' but trash noways.

"Oowee, boy!" Slapper shouted. " 'At's 'air's a fine idea, Jud. We could pull 'er in and run 'er through the search lak we used to. Ain't done 'at in a while. Then maybe we could convince 'er it'd be in Goldie's bes' interest for her to shake loose with some of that snatch. How long's it been since you had some young stuff, Jud?"

Manville had to think on that for a moment. He had him a little ol' high yellow gal back in the hills; but she was all swoll up pregnant. Come to think of it, he mused, it'd been a while since his wife give him any. Not that he really wanted anything from her.

"She clean?" Jud asked.

"Oh, man, yeah!" Slapper said. "Lak a new dime. " 'At's Luke's kid; you 'member her."

"Yeah. Sassy little ol' thing, as I recall. Twitchin' up and down the street. Ain't she got a sister, too?"

"Yeah. She's visitin' with Sue this weekend, too," the sheriff was informed.

"All right. Pull 'em both in. But I get first dibs, boys. My pick of the crop."

"Wouldn't have it no other way, Jud," Slapper said. "Claire's the sister's name. And she is shore a fine-lookin' piece."

Goldie began cussing them, screaming out his hate from the floor of the cell. He compared them all to that which was found on the floor of a bat cave.

His vocal rage was cut short with a howling cry of agony. Sheriff Manville had touched the cattle prod to his testicles and hit the juice.

Goldie screamed and rolled on the floor. Manville lifted the prod and touched the tip to Goldie's penis. Goldie's shrieking was hideous to hear. He tried to cover his swelling privates with his hands. The prod touched his naked thigh. The man tried to roll away from the agony. Manville shoved the tip between the man's buttocks and hit the juice. Goldie jerked in pain and screamed.

Everyone but Goldie thought it was hysterically amusing. They laughed and laughed at the sight.

Manville looked at one of his deputies. "Call Erin and have her come down here to be present during the search. We want this to be all legal-like, you know." He chuckled. "Then go get them gals!"

State police headquarters—earlier that afternoon

"You wanted to see me, sir?" The Kentucky Highway Patrol officer stepped into the colonel's office.

He was waved to a seat. "All right, Mac," Colonel Harrison said. "I want a straight answer from you, and no bullshit. You understand that, Mac?"

"Yes, sir," Major Mac Duncan replied, a puzzled tone in his voice. He'd been pulled out of the field for this, and from right off the bat, it didn't sound good.

"Now, I know you boys in intelligence don't always agree with my orders and decisions; but this time you've got too far with this ongoing Dane County investigation."

Mac sat and stared at him for a moment. "Sir, I don't know what you mean. What you're talking about. So far as I am aware, we have no investigation going on in Dane County. Not that there shouldn't be one," he added.

"Damn it, I said no bullshit, *Major!*" He leaned on Mac's rank.

Mac fired back his reply, not giving an inch. "You're not getting any bullshit, *Colonel.* And do forgive my impudence, *Colonel,* but I haven't the foggiest idea what you're talking about, *Colonel,* sir!"

Harrison sat back down in his chair, laughing. He wiped his eyes and fished in his pocket for a cigar, lighting up. "Sorry, Mac. But I had to come on that way; see if I could make you mad. Guess I succeeded, huh?"

"Rather well, sir. What is all this about Dane County?"

"Beats the hell out of me, Mac. Inspector Rogers was in here this afternoon. He got a call on that phone." He gestured toward his private line. "From Washington, I gathered. The way he was tippy-toeing around and whispering and acting jumpy, I figured he wanted me to leave. Tell you the truth, that pissed me off. So I just point-blank asked him if he wanted me to leave. He did! That really pissed me off. I wasn't dragging my feet leaving the office, but I wasn't playing Seattle Slew either." He puffed on his cigar for a moment.

The colonel blew a smoke ring and said, "I heard him say he hadn't had a word out of his agent in Anson. But the last thing he had heard was that something big was about to pop. I was out the door by then. You know about anything that's going down in Anson?"

"Not a thing. Nothing. And that sort of pisses me off, too. The Bureau usually coordinates with us. But I'll tell you what I do have: two men not forty miles from Anson. They're just returning from wrapping up that mess outside of Harlen. They're at a motel; called in about an hour ago. Told me they were beat. Wanted to rest some. All they have is walkie-talkies in their pickup."

Harrison nodded. "Call them. Send them in. If something is going on there, I want to know about it. Now I want you to listen to this." He punched the button on a cassette recorder. It was Inspector Rogers, speaking with Colonel Harrison.

"I assure you, Colonel, the inspector said. "There is nothing going down in Dane County. Nothing at all."

There was more chitchat. Again the man assured the colonel that nothing was taking place in Dane County. Absolutely nothing at all.

Harrison clicked off the machine. From the manner in which he punched the button, Mac had serious doubts the machine would ever work again. Harrison was highly irritated. "Lying through his teeth to me. Lying! But why?"

"It could be he's thinking we'd try to protect Tay

Blessing. That is, if Blessing is under any sort of investigation—and I hope the worthless bastard is."

"I wish somebody would shoot the son of a bitch!" Colonel Harrison said. "Yeah, you're right; that's my thinking on the matter. Cops do protect cops, that's a fact. But not that son of a bitch. He's the last of our political appointees, and I can't wait until he's gone." He shook his head and ashtrayed his stogie. "But I thought the Bureau knew the only reason Tay is still on our payroll is because of Maxwell Anson's power and influence."

Mac shrugged. "Maybe it goes much deeper than just one bad state cop."

Harrison arched one eyebrow. "Oh? You mean . . . Big Daddy himself?"

"Could be."

"Wouldn't that be deliciously wonderful? God, you know I despise Maxwell Anson more than I do Tay Blessing. Tay is ignorant; Maxwell knows better. I am on—ah—unofficial record as having said that Blessing wasn't worth the gunpowder to blow his brains out, and that he was a no-good, on-the-take, womanizing, prisoner-beating fuckhead!"

Mac laughed. "Yes, sir. I seem to recall something like that."

Harrison grimaced. "Yeah—and so did our governor at the time. Thank God, the people voted that prick out. I got called on the carpet good for that, but I stood by my comments."

"Dane County has always been a snake pit when it comes to law enforcement, decent record keeping, rigged elections. There isn't a decent cop in that county. They're all dipshits, and worse. Son Cody would like nothing better than to take his men in there and clean it up." The head of Intelligence sighed. "We've been so close, so many times, only to have it blocked by—"

"By someone in very high federal office who shall remain nameless." Colonel Harrison cut him short. "We don't mention that name aloud, Mac. But you know what I'm thinking?"

"Yes, sir. That, ah, federal officeholder." He smiled. "Wouldn't that be something?"

"That's almost too much to wish for. Mac, we've got a pretty good bunch of cops in this state. For the most part. It took us a while, but we made it. We'll have an even better group when Jud Manville and that pack of rednecks is gone, along with Maxwell Anson. And they will be gone, Mac; time is catching up with them. Maybe time *has* caught up with them. One can only hope."

"And one can only hope it's done without an accompanying bloodbath from the good citizens fed up with it."

"Yes. All right. What two do you have in the area?"

Mac grinned and Harrison groaned. "Jesus! Those two." Then the man had to smile. "Mac, level with me—how did those two hillbillies ever earn masters' degrees and still retain the ability to look, act, and talk like a couple of Kentucky's worst rednecks?"

Mac laughed aloud. "I don't know, Colonel. But that's what makes them so good at their work. People just don't think they have any sense at all."

Niven Simmons and Peter Mills were two genuine characters from the deep mountains of Kentucky; long, lean, tobacco-chewing, skinny drinks of water who sounded like two people who had never laid eyes on a book of any sort—much less possessed the ability to actually read one. But both were highly educated and skilled investigators. They traveled in a pickup truck that looked as though it might fall apart at any time—and occasionally did.

But that only happened when the one driving let the hammer down on the souped-up mill under the hood.

On any investigation, the two men were like bloodhounds. Some said they even resembled hound dogs. But not to their faces.

"All right, Mac, use my phone and get in touch with those two characters of yours. Do it right now, please. Get them into Dane County immediately. Especially Anson. Start there. But Mac"—he held up a warning finger—"caution is the word. Utmost caution. Tell them don't interfere in anything; this is obviously the Bureau's show; so let the Bureau handle it until they ask for our help. If the bureau is in there—and I stress *if*—it's probably big and ugly and nasty as hell."

"Yeah? Well, I can name five that fit that description perfectly."

"Oh?"

"Yes, sir. Banger, Whacker, Slapper, Eddie, and Bugger."

Colonel Harrison reached for his stomach medicine.

Twelve

"What do they have Goldie charged with?" Barry asked, knowing it was a stupid question. But maybe the answer would open Brenda's eyes a bit. Like so many people, she had looked at a great many things, but had actually seen very little.

Adam snorted. "Man," he said, "where you been? Oh. OK, I get you. This is for Miss Brenda's ears. All right. This is Dane County. The least populated, poorest, most isolated county in the state. We been cut off due to floods and slides more times than I can remember. You 'member, Brenda?"

She nodded.

"There ain't no law in this county except what Maxwell Anson tells Sheriff Manville to enforce. Good God, we've had state people in here, federal people in here, big-city do-gooder types—you name it, we've had them here. Didn't do a bit of good. Manville and Anson just cover up everything quicker than a cat covers up a mess, until the folks is gone, and then everything is right back the way it was."

"Adam." Brenda met his eyes. "I swear to you I never knew all this."

"I know you didn't. It isn't your fault. You tried to

walk down the middle. Them that do that get left alone."

"And those that walk on your side, Adam?" she asked.

"Well, mighty funny-odd things happen to them folks. They can't prove none of it was illegal, though."

"Such as, Adam?" She refilled their coffee cups.

"Houses get burned down. Cars and trucks get forced off the road. Folks go visitin' out of town and they get mugged, robbed, beat up; one man died he was whipped so bad. Dope gets stuck into folks' cars and trucks, and they do hard time. The women get raped. But can't nobody prove nothin' was done illegal 'cause it's their word against the law, and Anson owns the judge.

"So you see, Miss Brenda, there ain't but one way to break the stranglehold Maxwell and his kin and followers have on this county, and that's to kill him and his boys and them that follow them.

"Goldie? Hell, he's gettin' the livin' shit beat out of him right about now. If it hasn't already happened. And them that are doin' it are doin' it for just one reason: to try to draw us out, make our move. And if that damn trashy Jerry Ryan and Curt is in on it—and they are, bet on it—Goldie's gettin' worked over with a cattle prod right about now. On his"—he cut his eyes to Brenda—"privates."

She grimaced. "Adam, I knew things were bad, but not this bad. Not the way you're telling us. I can't believe so many of us have been so blind about things."

"Miss Brenda, no offense now, don't take what I'm goin' to say wrong—but you're from another part of the county. Your folks had a little standin' in the community. Some higher education. Well . . . it just isn't the same for a lot of us." He seemed to be groping for words.

"It's not the same for the rest of us. I know, I had two years of college. But I didn't like it. Came back to work the mines. Tried to change things. You see where that got me. You wanna help out, Mister Rivera—or whatever the hell your name is?"

"I'll try. People of affluence, be it monetary or educational, will, in all probability, if they walk down the middle of the road, not be terribly bothered by the Anson family."

Adam blinked. "Is that right?" But there was a twinkle in his eyes. "Whatever it was you said sounds 'bout right." He smiled. "The rest of us—well, it just seems like we don't count in the overall scheme of things."

"Careful now," Barry warned with a smile. "Your education is slipping through all the bullshit."

"Don't spread it around, Barry. It'd ruin my good reputation."

The young miner rose and walked away, out of the private dining area. Both Barry and Brenda noticed the butt of the .38 sticking out of the hip pocket of his worn jeans.

Brenda said, "I hope nobody tries to arrest him tonight."

Barry's eyes were thoughtful as he watched the man leave. "I don't know. I get the feeling he's hoping they will try."

"Tell me about those drug searches."

"Strip searches. They are humiliating and dehumanizing. And in many cases, probably most, they are totally unnecessary. It's law that all departments use a female matron to search women. It doesn't always work that way. I'm betting Dane County doesn't. One of these days the Supreme Court is going to pull their collective heads out of their asses and outlaw the god-damned things."

A light sprinkle of rain still fell, dotting the county, slicking the roads and streets. In the basement of the Dane County jail—an area that had proved time and again to be totally soundproof—Sue Harris bit back a sob at the sight of her husband, lying half-naked and half-conscious on the dirty cell floor.

She forced herself to look at him. She made no sound, keeping her face unreadable.

Goldie's penis and ball sacs were swollen grotesquely. A bucket of water was tossed on Goldie, rousing him. Sue's younger sister's fingers bit hard into her arm, the fear the girl felt transmitted through the touch.

Sue had a pretty good idea of what was in store for both of them.

Slapper Anson stood before her, a big grin on his hog face. "I always heard you Mahoney girls liked big cocks. Hell, baby, your man ain't got nothin' in the dick department."

Sue cut her eyes from her husband's to Slapper's ugliness. There was undisguised hate in her dark eyes. "It isn't the size of the boat, Mister Anson. It's the motion of the ocean that counts."

Several people, including Erin, laughed at Slapper's suddenly red face. He clenched his fists and muttered obscenely under his breath. He glared at Sue. "I'll 'member that, bitch. You'll see."

"Enough of this," Jud Manville said, reaching into

his pocket. His eyes flicked over the two women. Might be a tough night for them outside, but in here, it was gonna be a whang-dang-doodle of a good time.

Sue looked at the sheriff. "Why were we brought here, Sheriff Manville? And why has my husband been tortured?"

"Tortured, girlie? Hell, he ain't been tortured." He did his best to look insulted. "Goldie resisted arrest, that's all."

"Of course, Sheriff. Sure."

"Tell us the names of those involved in this here uprisin', girl. I want names, and when it's goin' down. You cooperate, and you all walk out of here."

"My husband, too?"

"Shore."

"She don't know anything!" Goldie said, struggling to sit up on the concrete floor. "Leave her alone, Sheriff!"

"Yeah, she do. You all a bunch of liars. You tell me, Sue, or it's goin' hard for your man yonder."

"I don't know anything, Sheriff."

Jud smiled and nodded at Jerry. The deputy, smiling, stepped into the cell and touched the cattle prod to Goldie's penis. The man screamed and flopped on the slick, wet floor. He fell back, stunned and hurting.

She fought inwardly to keep from screaming. Goldie's color was bad, and she didn't know how much more he could take.

Jud held out a plastic bag he'd taken from his pocket. The bag contained marijuana. "Found this in your car, Sue. Serious offense in this state. Gonna have to put you and your sis under arrest, I reckon. You and your sister, start strippin' down; gonna have to search you for other drugs."

Goldie groaned in his cell. "I'll tell you what you want to know, Manville. Just leavc my wife and her sister alone. Leave them alone, damn you!"

"Don't tell them anything, Goldie!" Sue cried. "You can't trust these people."

"I gotta, baby!" Goldie practically screamed the words. "They're gonna rape you both if I don't tell them."

Sudden understanding leaped into Sue's eyes. "No, Goldie. They're goin' to rape us no matter what you say." She looked into Jud's eyes, and something in her gaze caused the man to take a step backward.

"You better do what I tal' you to do, girl, "Jud warned.

"You and your men will have your way with us this night, Jud Manville." Sue never took her eyes off the man. "But it's over for you."

"Whut you mean, girl? Are you standin' there threatenin' me?"

"They'll kill you this night, Manville."

He slapped her, reddening her cheek. "Damn mincr trash slut. Strip 'em down, boys!" he yelled. "Right down to the hair and tits."

The women struggled, but it was useless and they both knew it. Claire was sobbing, the tears streaking her young face. Embarrassed, the women stood in front of the grinning group of men and Erin.

Erin said, "Bend over, Sue. Grab your ankles, baby." And Goldie's world began to fade as the sights and sounds around him intensified.

"Harry!" Sol Wiseman's eyes widened. "Harry!" He hugged his brother. "I can't believe my eyes. Why didn't you call and tell us you were coming? We'd have planned a celebration!"

"Does this town go to bed with the chickens, Sol?" Harry asked with a smile. "Nothing is moving."

"It's a quiet little town, Harry."

Was there something else in his brother's voice? Harry thought so. But maybe he was just tired, imagining things. That was probably it.

"Sol?" his wife called from the living room. "What is it?"

"It's my brother, Grace. Honest to God, it's Harry." His eyes penetrated the darkness, wet with mist, finding the two men with the brother he had not seen in several years. "And . . . friends, too."

Sol stepped back. "Your friends have names, Harry?"

"Sam and Oscar." Harry smiled, a slight curving of his lips.

"What? Your friends don't have last names?" Sol motioned them out of the foyer and into the living room.

"Smith," Sam said.

"Jones," Oscar said.

"And pigs fly." Sol laughed, rolling his eyes. "So, all right. Sam and Oscar is fine."

They all laughed.

Grace kissed her brother-in-law and commented that he was too thin. What did his wife feed him?

"We've been on the move a lot, Grace."

She didn't pursue that. "You're all just in time for dinner," she informed them, looking at the clock. "And where are the girls, Sol? It's past time for them to be home."

"They'll be here; they'll be here!" Sol patted her

arm. "You'll worry yourself into the grave. Nothing is going to happen to them."

"Ruth and Esther must be . . . well"—Harry paused—"sixteen and seventeen."

"Right on the mark!" Sol smiled, happy that his brother should remember. "And lovely. Both of them are beautiful."

"I'm sure they take after their mother," Sam said.

"I like him," Grace said, smiling.

"I was going to say the same thing," Oscar said quickly. "He just beat me to it."

Laughter brought them closer still.

"Why should anything happen to the girls?" Harry asked, puzzled at his brother's comment.

"It's nothing." Sol waved that away. "Believe me, it's nothing."

"I told you not to let them go out this afternoon, Sol. Things are—"

A dark look from the husband and the wife stopped in mid-sentence.

Harry, Sam, and Oscar looked at each other.

Something was definitely going on. "It's Saturday evening," Harry said. "The streets should be filled with people."

Sol shrugged. "Business is bad. I closed the store early. Nothing is wrong."

"You keep saying that," his brother reminded him.

Sol said nothing.

"I have presents," Harry said, breaking the silence.

Sol waved that aside. "You and your friends are presents enough." He looked more closely at his brother and friends. They were all burned dark from the desert sun and the hot winds. To a man they all looked fit—very fit. "You guys been eating trees, maybe?" Sol asked, conscious of his spreading middle and that he needed to lose ten pounds. Maybe fifteen.

"We still try to plant them, Sol."

"Uh-huh. So, Harry, you got tired of the army, maybe?"

His brother smiled. "Oh, no. Not really. We're here to train and lecture on a few bases. Make some speeches and new friends, hopefully."

Sol nodded his understanding. "I know, I know. Nothing ever changes. But if you think you're going to be welcomed with open arms here in this county . . ." He rolled his eyes and looked heavenward.

Harry and Oscar and Sam smiled. While they were all three quite human and knew the sensation of fear, they did not live with it on a day-to-day basis. All three were veteran soldiers, Israeli commandos. The men were veterans and heroes of the raid at Entebbe.

Colonel Harry Wiseman helped plan it.

None of the three saw absolutely any reason to be afraid of anything in Dane County.

Or anybody.

Thirteen

The thought had come to Sheriff Jud Manville that perhaps this time they had all lost their heads and gone too far. A man can do that over a piece of ass.

Goldie had passed out after that last jolt of juice from the cattle prod, and his breathing was funny; eyes rolled back in his head and drool leaking out from his mouth. His skin felt strange and clammy.

Well, men had died in his jail before and nothing had ever come of it.

Deputy Ben Gardner was scared and made no effort to hide that fact. It would have been useless anyway, he thought, embarrassed: he had pissed in his underwear. Oh, he knew these men around him, had gone to school with most of them. Grew up with them. But more importantly, he knew what they were capable of doing when they got riled up—and they were definitely riled up this night.

"What's happened to Goldie, Ben?" Adam Wallace asked. He slapped Ben's nightstick into the palm of his hand, punctuating his question with a dull pop.

"Come on, boy!" another man spoke. "Answer the question, you sorry Anson-ass-kisser."

The deputy looked at the nightstick. He wished Adam would stop slapping it against the palm of his hand. He wondered how that club would feel coming up hard against the side of his head. Like he'd done with so many people. Ben had him a pretty strong hunch that he wasn't all that far away from finding out.

Why in the hell, he thought, *didn't I have enough sense to get gone when I had the chance?*

The side of his head exploded in pain. Ben thought Adam had hit him with the club. But all he'd done was slap him.

"Answer the question, damn it!"

"Man, I don't know nothin' about Goldie! I ain't been to the station house in hours. I been on patrol since three o'clock this afternoon. Jesus, Adam—I'm tellin' you the truth."

"Adam?" a man spoke from out of the misty darkness. "Goldie's wife and her sister is missin'. Neighbors say a sheriff's car come and got them more than an hour ago. They didn't know where they took 'em."

"Let's storm the jail!" a man shouted.

"You know what's happenin' to Sue and Claire!" a woman shouted out of the knot of people. "Slapper's down at the jail."

"Let's rush the place!"

"No!" Adam shouted down the crowd of angry men and women. "Not unless y'all wanna commit suicide. Damn it, that's what they want us to do. Now, just settle down and listen to me—"

"We're tired of listenin', Adam!" His shout was flung back at him from within the growing crowd of armed men and women. "It's time to do it. Time for us to take back the town; make our move. We got the guns, we got the people. So damn it, let's do it."

"One more hour," Adam pleaded. "Just one more hour, that's all I ask. Let's find out for certain what's happened to Goldie and them and then, if something bad has happened . . . we'll do it."

He looked around for Lucas Webster. But the black minister had not made an appearance, and he was hours late already. That was not like Lucas. He had entirely too much riding on the outcome of all this. He was too heavily involved to pull back when they were so close.

The crowd talked among themselves for a moment. "All right, Adam," someone said. "One more hour. And I mean that. Just one hour. And then we do it with guns and we do it right this first time. After it's done, nobody knows nothin'."

Adam could only shake his head in agreement.

"Y'all better turn me a-loose," Deputy Gardner said, a warning note in his voice. "If you don't, it's gonna go hard for you all. Y'all are fuckin' up bad tonight."

Adam turned hard bright eyes on the deputy. "Some of you take this scumbag out to number five shaft," he ordered. "Lock him in. "He'll play billy-hell gettin' out of there."

Men moved closer to the deputy. Ben started sweating in the light mist.

"I think he's scared," a man spoke.

"You trashy bastard!" the deputy cursed Adam. "Boy, you lost what little sense you ever had. Mister Anson gets done with your ass you be down on your knees prayin' your mommy never whelped you."

At that insult to his mother, Adam swung the nightstick. The last thing Deputy Ben Gardner would remember for a good hour was: so this was how it felt to get popped with a nightstick.

* * *

"Get him out of here," Maxwell said wearily. "Rig some sort of automobile accident for Goldie and his wife. Get in touch with Tay and have him investigate it—quickly. Make it a bad one. Have the car burn. Damn it, Jud! I can't believe you did this. It's not like you. This is just plain stupid!"

"I guess we lost our heads, Mister Anson," Jud spoke into the phone. "Hell—I know I did. But it won't happen again."

"It's too late for self-recrimination, Jud. Come to think of it, it just may be too late for everything!" He slammed the phone down.

Maxwell Anson turned slowly in his expensive leather chair behind his huge oak desk in the study. He listened to the soft patter of rain falling against the study window. The thought came to him: It was all coming apart at the seams. A nearly one hundred and fifty year empire was cracking and crumbling and falling.

And as he sat, deep in thought, yet another thought sprang into his mind: Maybe it was time.

The town cop was just slightly less than belligerent, in both tone and bearing. "All right, Wiseman. You called for a cop; here one is. Now what's your little problem?"

Harry Wiseman lifted his suddenly narrowed eyes at the man's unfriendly tone. Sam and Oscar stirred slightly in their chairs. All knew the tone very well. And none liked it.

"It's my daughters, Officer," Sol patiently explained. "Ruth and Esther. They're both missing. More than two hours now. It isn't like them to be so late, and I'm afraid something has happened to them. We're all afraid of that."

The young cop grinned knowingly. "Well, that's no big deal, Wiseman. Happens all the time. You know kids. They probably went ridin' around with some young boys. You know."

"No, I don't know," Sol replied tolerantly. He knew what the officer was implying. Chose to ignore that. Sol was used to it. He didn't like it; but when in Rome and so forth.

Harry Wiseman liked it even less. A great deal less. He felt like getting up and slapping the piss out of the smart-mouthed cop. But he was in the town his brother had chosen to live in . . . and that was another mystery to Harry. He mentally cooled his temper, banking the fires, and said, "Exactly, Officer, what *are* you implying about Ruth and Esther?"

The young cop, and in fairness, he did not know what was taking place in the jail, or what had happened to the Wiseman girls, opened his mouth to pop off. He closed it abruptly as Harry picked that time to stand up. Big dude. Solid. Looked mean. Face like old leather. Hard, flat eyes. But the city cop figured he had the badge and gun and Maxwell Anson behind him. He knew the only reason Mister Anson let Wiseman stay in business was 'cause he didn't cause no trouble and didn't get sassy with real white folks.

The cop spread his feet and took a deep breath. "I mean, mister—not that it's any of your business—that the girls probably found themselves a couple of boys and went off into the woods to fool around; that's what I meant."

Harry stepped closer. The cop took a better look at

the man. Jesus, the guy was hard-lookin'. Dangerous lookin', even.

"I don't like what you're implying, Officer," Harry spoke softly. "Not a bit. Tell me, do you always speak in such an insulting tone to my brother and his wife?"

Brother? Oh, boy. "Ah—hey!" The young cop's face flushed. Then he remembered he didn't have a backup outside. "Look, mister, nobody asked for none of your mouth. So why don't you just close it and butt out, OK?"

"No," Harry said.

"Haw?"

"I said no. I have no intention of butting out of this matter. Your move, Officer."

"I gotta live here, Harry," Sol softly reminded his brother."

"No, you don't, Sol. That's crap and you know it. You've been saying that for so long you're beginning to believe it. Don't. There is always a place for you with us, and don't ever doubt that."

He had not taken his eyes off the young cop as he spoke. "Are you going to look for my nieces, or do we . . ." He indicated his two friends, standing nearby.

The cop took a close look at the two friends. They all had the same expression; a flat, no-nonsense look about them. They looked, well—the cop struggled for a word to describe the tanned, lean-looking men—like . . . warriors, he finally decided.

"Hey, ah . . . are you guys in the army, or something?" he asked.

"You might say that," Oscar spoke up.

The cop looked around; he was boxed in, and it had been done expertly. And quietly. He could not move more than two or three inches in any direction. "Where are you guys stationed?"

"Israel," Harry told him. There was an amused look in his eyes. The cop looked at Sam and Oscar. They had the same amused look in their eyes.

"The . . . Israeli Army?"

"That is correct."

Even in Dane County most folks had heard of that army. Unless they lived in a tree back in the deep timber. Don't fuck with the Jews. They kick ass. Hard.

"You, ah, you guys some sort of, ah, special troops, maybe?"

Standard joke around the station house, back when that nutbrain took all the hostages in Iran, grabbing the embassy, was that President Carter should have got on the horn with Begin and worked out a deal: we pay you, you go in and get our people.

Whole thing would have been over in twenty-four hours. Maybe less.

"Commandos," Sam told him.

"Is that right?"

"That is correct."

"That there's a real good outfit."

"We think so," Oscar replied.

"Well—if y'all will excuse me, I'll just go lookin' for your daughters, Mister Wiseman."

"That would be very kind of you, Officer," Sol said.

"Think nothin' of it. Just doin' my job." *Have to pass the word around; be a little bit nicer to Mr. and Mrs. Wiseman and kids. 'Cause Wiseman's brother and buddies look like they ate nails. And spit out bullets.* "Yes, sir. Always glad to oblige."

"We might drive around town ourselves," Harry said. "If that's all right with you, Officer?"

"Oh, yeah! Be fine. I'll get on the horn and tell the P.D. and the S.O. boys that you'll be around, and—to leave you alone." Damn sure tell them to do that. "Ah—you guys—ever . . . I mean, you killed lots of them sand niggers?"

"I beg your pardon, young man?" Harry glared at him.

"A-rabs."

"I find the term 'nigger' to be most offensive, Officer."

"Right! Me, too. Just sort of slipped out. Sorry. I'll be gettin' along now. I see your girls, Mister Wiseman, I'll shoo them on home quick-like."

"Thank you, Officer," Sol said.

"Would you like a piece of cake, Officer?" Grace asked.

"Ma'am?"

"It's fresh baked. Wait, I'll get you a piece and you can take it with you." She was back in half a minute with a piece of cake that would choke a Clydesdale. The cop thanked her and stepped out on the porch.

He looked back at the closed door. He felt a little funny-odd. The house wasn't at all like he'd expected. Come to think of it, he hadn't really known what to expect. He had thought there'd be all sorts of weird things around. Like what, he didn't know: But there wasn't. Just like anybody else's house. And the folks was just like anybody else. Nice people.

"I'll just be goddamned," he muttered. Took a bite of cake. Good cake, too."

He wondered where the girls might have gotten off to.

* * *

"I got a feeling, Harry," Sam said.

"Oh?"

"Like what I told you when we drove through town."

Harry looked at Oscar. The man nodded his head. "Same here, Colonel."

"All right. Sam, you stay here with Sol and Grace. I'll take Oscar; look around. Try the sheriff's department. They might know something."

The dispatcher at the jail looked at Harry's I.D. and felt something cold begin to work its way up his spine. He was going to have to lie to this man, and for the life of him, he knew there wasn't no way in hell he was gonna be convincing. He looked into Harry's eyes and went all cold inside.

He had been a cop all his life; now he was too old to do anything except handle the desk and the radio. But in his time, Clint had seen many of Kentucky's really bad old boys; he had known the feuders and the fussers and the fighters and no small number of outlaws down through the years. He knew it was always in the eyes: look in the eyes first. From the shifty-eyed homicidal maniacs to the cool bad ones. It was always in the eyes. And Colonel Harry Wiseman of the Israeli Army was a mighty bad one.

The chill in Clint turned to sweat as he lied. "Sorry, Colonel. I don't know nothin' 'bout these girls. Wish I could help you."

"Thank you very much, Deputy."

"You're shore welcome."

Outside, the rain had changed again to a light mist. Oscar said, "The old man is lying, Colonel. But why?"

"I know. And I'm getting the feeling that trouble is building all around us."

"I am sensing the same."

"Do you think we should take the chance and arm ourselves?"

"The Americans have an expression that fits that question very well."

"Oh?"

"Does a bear shit in the woods?"

Harry smiled. "The American soldiers are going to corrupt you yet, Major Frankel."

"Goddamnit, Jud!" the deputy said defensively. "They seen us carryin' out Goldie's body and heard them damn cryin' women. I don't know what in the hell they was doin' out back of the jailhouse; but they was there. They seen us. What else was I supposed to do, Sheriff?"

He walked to the girls. Looked down at the Wiseman kids. *Goddammit,* he silently cursed.

"We were taking a shortcut home from the movies, Sheriff," Esther said. "We stayed too long and we were late. We wanted to hurry."

Jud Manville nodded his head.

"May we leave now?" Ruth asked.

"In a minute, kids." Sheriff Manville felt a sinking sensation in the pit of his stomach, as he looked at the frightened girls. It's coming unglued, he thought. And that thought hit him hard, almost putting the man into a panic. For he knew very well that he was looking at spending the rest of his life in prison if a hard investigation ever took place in Dane County.

The Wiseman girls were crying and trembling. And

to make matters worse, Whacker Anson was leering at them. Jud knew what Whacker had on his mind.

"I want to go home now, Sheriff," Ruth said. "I want to call my parents and have our father come and pick us up. Could I do that, please?"

Pretty girls, too, Jud thought. Real pretty girls. Budding out right well, too. Curvy. But they seen too much. Couldn't let them live. A pity. If only the deputy hadn't panicked. He could have told them anything and they would have believed it. Drunks being took home. Anything. But instead, he lost his cool. A pity.

"Sheriff," Esther said, "could we please call our parents now?"

"We'll see that you get home, kids," Jud assured them. He looked at Whacker. The man was standing there like an ape, licking his lips. Jud could practically hear his evil thoughts. *But how much more evil is he than me,* Jud thought. He sighed. "Whacker, take the girls home, please."

"Shore be a pleasure, Sheriff." Whacker grinned. "An' I'll sure take 'em . . . straight home. 'Deed I will do that little thing."

"We want to go home, Mister Anson," Esther said. "Home! Now." She had stopped crying; did not appear to be afraid.

"Don't you git uppity with me, gal!" Whacker said.

"I am not being uppity with you, sir. I just don't understand why we're being detained so long. And I want to go home."

Whacker's eyes lingered on her breasts. He could practically sense how soft her body would be. How she would behave when he socked it to her. He was getting a hard-on. He smiled at her. "Why, shore! Let's go . . . home."

* * *

Filth was rolling out of Slapper's mouth as he hunched against the teenager's buttocks. "Now tell me that ain't gettin' good to you, girl?" he panted.

Claire sobbed her reply. She was drifting in a sea of hurt, an ocean of confusion and humiliation and tears. She had no idea what had happened to Sue. Only that they had been separated and taken away in different cars. She was afraid Sue was going to be killed.

And she was alternately afraid of being killed and fearful that she wouldn't be killed. At times she felt that death would be better than this.

"Slapper?" she heard a man ask. "Don't you reckon that some of us oughta be gettin' back to town? See what Adam and his bunch is up to. I thank so."

"Hell, no!" Slapper never missed a beat. "Them ol' boys at the Hall can take care of anything that comes up. Man, the way I feel right now, I can go all night." He patted Claire's bare back. "Don't you, baby?"

Claire chose not to reply.

She raised her head, looking at the room filled with grinning, half-naked and half-drunk men. She looked through a blur of tears and pain. She wished she was not in this particular position; the wooden sawhorse was rough against her belly and her legs were trembling from fatigue. She cried out in pain as Slapper continued his perversion.

The men called out for him to do this, that, and the other thing to her. She hoped none would happen. But she felt that it would.

And it did.

Somehow, she knew Slapper was grinning.

To make matters worse, if that was possible, she didn't even know where she was. She'd been shoved to the floorboards and held there, while hard hands did disgusting things to her.

Claire wanted to scream and curse at the men. But she knew that would only make matters worse for her. She didn't know what else could be done to her.

She would soon discover, along with a couple of other teenagers, that perversion took many forms. None of them pleasant.

She could see, through her tears, a pile of filthy mattresses lying about the room.

She wondered if the men were going to rape her on those nasty things?

They were.

She wondered if all of them were going to rape her.

Yes.

She wondered how long this would continue.

Many hours.

"Cars comin' in," someone said.

"Who is it?" Slapper asked, never missing a stroke.

"Your brother. And he's got them Wiseman gals with him, too. Pretty things."

"Hell's fire, boys!" Slapper yelled. "We're gonna have us a party tonight. Hammer and them don't know what they're a-missin'!"

"Yeah. I'd rather screw than fight any ol' time."

"Boys," a calmer voice said. "Do any of y'all know what we're gonna do with these gals onst we're finished with 'em?"

"Worry 'bout that later," Slapper said. "I wanna take me a poke at them Jew gals. I always figured they was hot to trot."

Claire felt him pull away from her. She sighed with

relief. She didn't know whether to straighten up from the sawhorse or not.

She did not have to ponder that for long. Another man took his place. And the rape continued.

Through her misty blur of pain and tears, she could see Ruth and Esther shoved into the large room. Esther looked at Claire and began screaming hysterically. She was forced to the floor, her clothing ripped from her. Another man was slapping Ruth, tearing her clothes away.

"Party time, boys!" someone yelled.

Fourteen

In the main auditorium of the First Baptist Church of Anson, a group of forty-odd men sat and talked. Various merchants, businessmen, mechanics, couple of lawyers, bank personnel, insurance agents, real estate people.

All with direct ties to Maxwell Anson and/or his many enterprises.

Including the minister.

"Somebody killed about ten men out to Anson's garage," a man spoke. "And all of a sudden it was hushed up."

"Ain't neither," another man said. "Sheriff Manville just turned it over to Tay Blessing to work on."

Many in the group laughed at that and the man flushed in anger. He decided to keep his mouth shut.

A wise move, considering the mood of the men attending the gathering.

Another man stood up among the pews. "Now look. Let's stop tippy-toeing around and spit it out. We've got to realize that if we fail, we all will be finished in Dane County. And starting over at our age is going to be a damn rough go."

"I don't think we have a choice," a service-station operator said.

Almost all agreed with him.

"How in the name of God did we, could we, allow conditions to get this far out of hand?"

" 'Cause we had it good and turned our heads away, refusing to see what was really happenin' around us, all the time," a man summed it up. "Makes me plumb ashamed of myself."

And almost all agreed with that.

"Sickenin'," a man was heard to mutter.

Willie Jefferson's daughter, Lisa Mae, had died, but not before mumbling to the lone nurse in her room what had happened; or at least enough of it for the nurse to put the rest of it together. The nurse lived in Anson. Her father was the Baptist minister.

The nurse had come straight home to her father, in tears, not knowing what to do with the information, but so shocked and horrified she felt she had to tell him what the Anson boys had done.

Her father had sat for a long time in his study at the church, in numbed silence. Brother Edmund Reed had known, of course, of the sexual antics of the Anson children; knew the offspring of Maxwell were all somewhat less than good Christian moral men and women. But he had always dismissed the rumors as just that—rumors—and no more than that. Then the realization that he—like so many others—had been deliberately deluding himself for years, struck him a hammer blow in the conscience. And it was not a feeling the minister liked . . . at all.

It had made him sick; violently sick to his stomach. He had thrown up several times.

He then had prayed to God for guidance; prayed all afternoon, then had called this meeting.

Edmund looked around the interior of the church;

gazed at all the opulence—provided, of course, by Maxwell Anson—and then thought about the little girl, now cold in death.

He watched as the owner of a large supermarket stood up. "Shirley Jefferson says she don't know where her husband is. She told me, all in tears, he taken a rifle and a pistol and was gone . . . somewhere."

It was starting, Edmund thought. The night was going to run red with blood. Rage had taken over. A night of rage.

"Maxwell has called in that bunch of rednecks and roughnecks he uses for strikebreakers," another voice added to the quiet confusion that currently reigned in the House of God. "They're all gathered over to the Hall. Erin Ramsey and Jane Causey and Jennifer Anson and a few other—ah, ladies, are with them. The Lord alone knows what's happening over there this night."

"I think we all have a pretty good idea," Brother Reed said, his voice as dry as a summer wind in Kansas. "Does anybody know if Anson has armed this bunch of trash?"

"To the teeth," he was informed.

"Several strangers prowlin' around town," Jack Miller said, standing up. Jack owned the big hardware store in town, and would, for a few more hours, at least. "First that truck driver fellow shows up. Mean-lookin' man; big man, with wrists on him like a roust-about. He's been nosin' around and keepin' company with Brenda Hooks." Jack smiled. "But a man can't fault him none for doin' that.

"Next some kin of Sol Wiseman shows up. Old Clint down at the sheriff's office called me and told me about him. The man's a colonel in the Jewish army.

Two hard-lookin' ol' boys with him. That come from a city cop. Goldie Harris was arrested on some trumped-up charge, and his wife and her sis was taken into jail. Now they're all disappeared.

"Ruth and Esther Wiseman didn't come home from the showhouse; Grace is about to go out of her mind. Sol had to put her to bed and call the doc to come give her a shot to knock her out.

"And now we got two ol' boys lookin' and talkin' like they just come down from a cave in the mountains showin' up in a ragtag old pickup truck. But Sidney down at the service station over on Willow Drive says he seen two nickel-plated .357's in holsters layin' on the floorboards of the truck. Said it looked to him like cop leather. But that isn't all."

How much more can there be, Brother Reed pondered.

He was about to find out. And before this night was over, he was to learn more about man's savagery than he had ever wanted to learn.

"Adam Wallace and a whole bunch of men—and some women—all armed, have gathered up at the West Fork. Word got back to me that Hammer Kearn is supposed to have said he was gonna kill Lucas Webster, and Lucas has disappeared, too. Deputy Gardner was last seen in a car with Johnny Springer and Henry Castine—headin' toward the timber. Gardner has disappeared.

"Boys," Jack said, looking around, "all those rumors we've been hearin' was true. We were fools to dismiss them. This town is fixin' to blow up in our faces. We'd better get off the dime and see what we can do to prevent it, or"—his face hardened—"pick one side and stay with it." He turned to Mayor Bradley. "Charlie, if you've got any influence with Maxwell Anson, you'd better do something and do it damn quick! Excuse my language, Brother Reed."

The mayor wore a confused look on his face. He spread his hands. "Everything was going so smoothly. What in the world happened?"

"What maybe happened was when you and Bugger and Eddie, or some of them damned trashy Anson boys, raped Johnny Springer's little girl!" The damning accusation was tossed at Mayor Bradley.

"That's a damned lie!" Bradley jumped to his feet. "All that was was just a vicious rumor, and you know it. All of you."

"No, it ain't, Charlie. Stop kiddin' yourself. You been likin' little girls and young boys—for a good many years now. We all knew about it."

"What!" Edmund Reed exploded, looking startled. "What about young girls and boys?"

"It's just a damned vicious lie!" Charlie Bradley screamed, jumping up and down. His face was flushed and he was trembling.

"Aw, hell, Charlie. You was caught playin' with that little Meeker boy back some years ago. The whole town knows you lean both ways. But we still elected you mayor, didn't we?"

"But you won't be elected no more," he was told. "Not since we learned of your taking part in the rape of that little girl."

"What—what—" Brother Edmund Reed stuttered.

"Liar! Liar! Liar!" Charlie Bradley screamed. "It's all just a vicious pack of lies. I'll sue you all for this."

"But you're a deacon in this church!" Brother Reed yelled at the man. "You teach a Sunday School class of little—" He broke it off, staring at the mayor.

Bradley stepped out into the aisle. He shook his finger at Reed. "So you men are going to side with the mine trash and the filth of this county against Maxwell Anson? Well, you'll all be damned sorry when you do, let me tell you that right now."

"You best carry your ass on out of here, Bradley." A man stood up, warning the mayor. "Somebody's liable to take a notion to kick it out the door."

"Don't you speak to me like that, you goddamned ignorant hillbilly!" The mayor puffed up, his fleshy jowls quivering.

Brother Edmund Reed walked up the center aisle of the church, toward the mayor. "You may leave now, Bradley. Leave this church building and consider your name forever removed from membership in His body of worship."

Bradley faced the minister, sticking out his chest. It was a futile gesture; his big belly got in the way. "What'd you say to me, you pipsqueak?"

"I said to take your cowardice and your hypocrisy and your sickening perversions and get the hell out of this church!" the minister thundered.

"Give him what-for, Preacher!" a man shouted.

"Why . . . you simperin' little shitass!" Bradley roared. "You can't talk to me like that! I'll have your skinny little ass run clear out of this county." He shook his finger in the preacher's face. "You sorry excuse for a man. You—"

Edmund Reed was standing close to the mayor when he executed a near-perfect right cross. Much to the amazement of both men and the gathering.

The impact of fist against mouth sent the mayor sprawling in the center aisle. He hit the carpet cussing, blood leaking from his busted lips. He grabbed for the side of a pew and missed in his haste, landing on his ample butt.

The gathering sat in silence for a few seconds, shocked by this act of violence from a man all considered to be one of the most gentle men in the town. Finally, one man said, "Preacher shore knocked him stiff, didn't he?"

Brother Reed smiled and rubbed his knuckles. "My, but that felt good," he said with satisfaction. "Brings to mind when I was a paratrooper in Korea."

The men all looked at each other. The preacher, a paratrooper? Nobody knew that.

The minister watched as Mayor Bradley struggled to get up. The preacher just couldn't resist putting one size-ten shoe on Bradley's butt and shoving. Bradley went down again, landing on his face on the carpet. He cussed the Baptist preacher.

"You son of a bitch!" Bradley cussed him. "You'll pay for this outrage."

"If you get up, Bradley," Edmund warned him. "I will knock you down again. And if you continue cursing me, I shall be sorely tempted to kick your damn face in while you're down."

"Well, how am I 'sposed to get gone?" Bradley squalled.

"Crawl like the poisonous reptile you are," the preacher advised him.

Bradley closed his mouth and began hunching up the aisle, getting to his feet in the anteroom and running out into the night.

Brother Reed turned to the men in the church. "I won't apologize for my actions or words. I may be a preacher, but I'm still a man."

"Amen to that!" several men said.

"Now, hear me," Brother Reed raised his voice. "Ecclesiastes shows us the way. There is a time for everything. Go home, arm yourselves, and meet me back here at the church. All those who have the courage to stand up for what is right and to combat the evil we have all known existed in this county for too long.

"We have all heard the horror stories of things that have taken place in the Dane County jail; we refused to believe them. Well . . . if just one percent of those stories have a ring of truth to it—and they're probably all true—we've waited much too long to act. We've been cowards, all of us. Now it's time for us to take a good hard look at ourselves, in the mirrors of our souls, and make up our minds whether we shall spend the rest of our lives fishing or cutting bait!"

The men rose and filed silently out of the church, heading home to get their deer rifles and duck guns and pistols. They were of a single mind.

And the lid blew off of Dane County.

Fifteen

"I think it's time," Barry told Brenda. "I want you to go to your quarters, take your pistol with you. Lock and bar the door. Now go on. You—"

"No!" She stuck out her chin.

"Brenda, don't be a damn fool. You don't know what you're letting yourself in for. I've seen riots. Seen what happens when good people lose control and run wild. They become savages."

"I'm sticking with you, Barry."

He smiled. "You know what I'm going to do, Brenda?"

She shook her head.

"I'm going to pull my rig up as close to the motel as I can, tuck it in tight, and stay right here!"

"It's the only way, Mister Anson," Tay Blessing told the man.

Maxwell sighed heavily. If he went along with Tay's plan, he'd be digging his own grave with a silver spade. And the hole was getting deeper and deeper. Soon, he knew, there would be no way out. He had to think; had to find the time to think. He shook his head.

"A lot of killing, Tay. Just too much killing."

"No way to prove nothin' if they can't find no bodies, sir," the maverick highway cop said.

Someone hammered on the front door of the mansion. A shout, then muffled voices from the hall. Footsteps, in a hurry, almost running. The study door was flung open. Mayor Charlie Bradley lunged into the room, his hair a mess, his mouth bloody.

"My God, Charlie!" Maxwell half rose from his chair. "What happened?"

"You look like someone just beat the hell out of you," Tay said.

Bradley waved them both silent and stumbled toward the wet bar. He poured a stiff glass of booze and gulped it down. He poured another and walked to a chair beside Maxwell's desk, sitting down heavily.

He rubbed his face and said, "Comin' apart, boys. Ever'thing." He told them about the meeting at the church, then sat quietly for a time, letting the men absorb it all.

Charlie said, "I'm gettin' out of here. We lost. Y'all better cut and run; 'cause if them people find you, way they's all riled up, they'll kill you both . . . after they tar and feather you. Or worse." He rose from the chair and walked slowly toward the door. With his back to the men, he said, "See you, boys." The door closed behind him.

"He's just scared shitless," Tay said contemptuously. "Damn fat fag!"

Maxwell wasn't so sure of Bradley's fright. The man just might be right. He leaned back in his chair and closed his eyes. He pursed his lips reflectively and was silent in thought for several minutes.

Tay waited; had a hunch what was going on in Maxwell's mind. Tay was doing some thinking of his own.

Finally Maxwell opened his eyes and met the gaze of Tay. "It's over. I will not be a part in any further cover-up. I have allowed myself to be trapped by my children's ignorance . . . and, I admit, by my own greed. I have been a party, both knowingly and after the fact, to crimes. Brutal ones of late. But no one can directly connect me to any killings. And I want it stopped before any more occur."

Tay waited; his thinking had been correct.

Maxwell said, "I will take my chances in a court of law. Any charges against me—my attorney can delay for months, maybe even years. I have the best attorneys in the state at my disposal. My sons and daughter, and I think they are borderline insane, can use that defense. I will pay for your defense, Tay. But it's over. Right now. It's all over."

Tay waited. He had his own plans, and they damn sure included Maxwell Anson. He wasn't about to go down without a fight, and he'd damn sure take this smug bastard with him.

"No," Maxwell spoke softly. "On second thought, I'll order my car sent around. I'll leave the country for a time. Perhaps forever. I don't know what the hell I'll do. I need time to think. I have extensive holdings in South America. God, I'm so tired and so confused."

There was an odd, savage look in Tay's eyes. Murder in his mind. Revenge. "So you're just tossing us all to the dogs, huh, Maxwell?"

"Call it what you will, Blessing. I told you: I need time to think and time is running out. Time has run out. For now, I want you to leave. Just get out." He spun in his chair, putting his back to the cop. "Right now, Tay. Leave me alone. I need time."

Something cold and hard touched the millionaire's neck. Maxwell did not have to turn around to know what it was. A pistol. He remained very still as the cop jacked back the hammer.

"Don't be a fool, Blessing. Without my backing, you'll go to prison. Think about that before you do something that you'll always regret. Think about it, Blessing."

Tay laughed. A nasty laugh. "I been thinkin' on it, Anson. I figured if things went sour, you'd cut and run; leave us all for the wolves. But I got news for you, Mister Hot-Shit Fancy Pants. If we go down, you sure as hell are goin' down with us. All the way down hard."

"I doubt it," Maxwell replied arrogantly. "I really do doubt it."

"I don't. Get up," Tay ordered. He removed the muzzle of the .357 from Anson's neck. "Get up slow and easy. I won't kill you, but I'll damn sure knock a leg out from under you."

Maxwell rose to his feet. Oddly, he felt no fear. Yet. "What are you going to do, Tay?"

The cop grinned. "Why, sir, first off, you gonna get you some young nookie. Yes, sir, Maxwell. You don't mind if I call you Maxwell, do you? Good. You're gonna screw you a minor. And you're gonna do it willingly, knowingly, and as we say, of your own volition. Yes, sir. You are going to take part in a rape."

"And I will certainly refuse to do that. Now what, Blessing?"

"Oh, you're gonna do it, Maxwell. You're gonna get it hard and screw a kid."

"I doubt it. And if I don't? What then, Blessing?"

"Why—then I tell the boys down at the hall and out at the warehouse what you was plannin' on doin'. You ever been cornholed, Maxwell?"

"Certainly not!"

"Well, don't give up hope. Them ol' boys you got on your payroll, the ones you use to bust heads, is randy and mean. They'll do anythin'. And then, after they get through with you, I'll tell it all to the law. I'll tell the law—and the boys will back me up—that everything was your idea; that you ordered it all: the murders, the rapes, the cover-ups—everything. But it'll be fun watchin' you get reamed, Maxwell. Yes, sir. You might be a four-ten goin' in, but when them ol' boys get through with you, you'll be a twelve gauge comin' out. If you get my drift."

He did.

It started with the smashing of a window of Maxwell Anson's bank building. Then somebody tossed a can of gasoline into the bank. A match followed. The fumes exploded, blowing out all the windows and killing two citizens standing in front of the bank. The two men who had thrown the gas and the match.

Their charred and broken bodies were left in the street.

"Knock out the phones!" somebody yelled over the whine and howl of fire trucks.

A shot was fired at the trucks and they stopped dead in the street, out of the line of fire. The bank building became an inferno.

"Get some dynamite and caps and blow the phone building!" a woman screamed. "The night is ours!"

It was not clear then and never would be just who yelled what on that night of violence and bloody rage in Anson.

"We got the roads blocked!" a miner yelled. "No one comes in or goes out unless the boys OK 'em." Sirens screamed in the background. "Let's go, boys!" He waved his hand just as the young city cop who had responded to the Wiseman call squalled his unit to a halt across the street from the burning bank building. He still had a few cake crumbs on his shirt-front.

"What the hell is goin' on here?" the cop yelled, backing up from the intense heat from the burning bank. "You people clear the street and let the fire trucks get in here. Stand over there across the road. What the hell are you people doin' with all them guns?"

He put his hand on the butt of his pistol. A rifle cracked. The young officer doubled over and went down screaming as the 7mm mag slug tore a great hole in his stomach. He lay dying on the sidewalk.

"Help me!" he screamed.

No one came to his aid. If you wore a cop's uniform, you were the enemy; because you worked for Maxwell Anson.

"There ain't no turnin' back now, people!" a woman yelled. "Come on. Let's do it right."

"Yeah!" a man yelled from out of the firelit night. "Let's get them."

One of the more sensible members of the now unmanageable and furious mob muttered, "Get who?"

No one answered the question.

* * *

Deputy Sheriff/FBI Agent Granger Kildare slid to a stop at the sound of the first violent explosion. Gunshots followed right on the heels of the booming roar and the flames that rocked and leaped into the misty night sky. He ran for a phone; far down the street he could see shadowy figures of the mob as they moved, marching along in rough military formation, several hundred strong, toward the Hall where the Anson roughnecks were drinking and partying.

More shots were fired, those coming from the opposite end of town.

"Oh, hell!" Granger muttered, stepping to the pay phone and fumbling for change. He fed the coins into the slot and punched out the number. The phone started ringing at the other end. The wait seemed endless. About five seconds.

The marching mob drew closer, their ranks swelling with each block.

"Federal Bureau of Investigation," the man said.

Granger knew the voice; it belonged to Agent Drew Ryan. "Drew!" He shouted the word. "Granger here. Listen to me. It's coming apart. I—"

The line went dead.

"Oh, fuck!" Granger shouted, sending Herbert Hoover spinning in his grave, since FBI agents were not supposed to use gutter language.

Granger slammed the receiver back into the cradle and ran for his car, driving away from the shouting and murderous mob.

As he drove to a higher and, he hoped, safer ground, he wondered if God really heard all prayers. If so, he silently spoke to the Big Agent in the sky, would You please send in the nearest battalion of

Army Rangers . . . combat equipped, if You don't mind?

"Hi, there, Daddy!" Whacker bellowed drunkenly as Maxwell entered the room of rape and perversion and debauchery. "Whut you say, Tay?"

"Your poppa decided he'd like to have some of that young stuff tonight," Tay said with a grin. "He was plumb insistent about it. Which one of them gals is the best? That little blonde gal looks to be wore slap out to me."

"Well, come on in, Daddy!" Slapper laughed. "Hell, we can always go back to town and grab us up some other gals. We glad to see you. Hell, there ain't nobody gonna do nothin' to us—we Ansons, right?" He looked around. "You there, Jody—bend that Jew gal over."

Maxwell Anson felt sick to his stomach. All eyes in the room were on him as his son's words echoed in his brain: "Ain't nobody gonna do nothin' to us—we Ansons."

God, what have I done?

The men were laughing and cursing profanely and passing bottles of booze around.

This is not happening to me, Maxwell thought, wanting desperately to believe it. *This just* can't *be happening to me!*

But he knew it was, and it was too late to look back and wish and hope. Kind of like sitting in a dentist's chair and wishing you had taken better care of your teeth; maybe you wouldn't be there.

But you were, and your tooth was aching

"Step out of your fancy pants, Fancy Pants," Tay

whispered from behind him. "That pretty dark-haired gal is waitin' for you to pop it to 'er. So get to pokin', Maxwell."

"And if I refuse?"

"You gonna get poked."

Maxwell loosened his belt, his trousers dropping around his ankles. He peeled down to his underwear. He turned his head and whispered, "What about the situation in town?"

"Bad. Looks like we gonna lose. Roads is blocked. You heard it on the radio comin' out here same as I did. So we're all goin' down together. But they gonna be fightin' all night. Get to humpin', Maxwell."

"Wonderful," Maxwell said dryly.

The men were all clapping their hands and urging him on.

Maxwell experienced many emotions as he walked across the dirty floor. He walked up to the sawhorse to stand behind the teenager. She looked up at him, tears in her brown eyes.

"Please, Mister Anson. Don't. Stop this. You've known me and my sister all our lives. You used to give me candy when I'd come into the bank with Daddy."

"You a big girl, now!" Whacker yelled. "Daddy gonna give you somethin' to celebrate your comin' of age and all 'at."

"Yeah," Jody laughed. "This be your cotillion party for young ladies."

"Do it, Daddy!" Eddie yelled.

All right, Maxwell thought. *I've got the best lawyers money can buy. They can convince a jury I was forced to do this thing.*

"Go, Daddy!" Whacker screamed.

"Do it, Daddy!" Eddie hollered.

Daddy did it.

The girl started screaming.

"Stand up and stand aside," Brother Edmund Reed said. He backed up his words with a lever-action .30-30 rifle.

"Brother Reed!" the old dispatcher said, astonishment in his voice. And some fear in there as well.

"None other, Clint," the preacher's voice and hands were calm and steady. "Don't do anything rash. Just answer the questions I ask."

"Don't you worry about that," Clint assured him. "Whatever you say, Preacher. Just don't get antsy and tighten up that trigger figger—ah, trigger finger."

"Where is Sheriff Manville?"

"Lord, Lord, Brother Reed—I don't know." The old man's words were pleading. He rose carefully and slowly from behind the desk. "Brother Reed, have you lost your mind?"

"Rather, Clint, I believe I have just found it after a long period of years."

"And the rest of us as well, Clint," Jack Miller spoke from the open doorway as he stepped inside. He held a twelve-gauge shotgun in his hands. "The town of Anson is coming apart, Clint. The people are in revolt against Maxwell Anson and his trashy sons."

"So I been hearin'. And y'all a part of it, huh, boys?"

"You got that right, Clint."

"Now, boys." Clint tried to calm what he knew was a situation that could get him seriously dead quicker than Johnny Cash could change harmonicas. "Now—

y'all just wait a minute. Maybe things ain't been all to your likin'. But for God's sake, step back some and think about what you're doin'. How about it, fellows?"

"We are ending Maxwell Anson's reign of terror," the minister announced. "And we are doing it right now—tonight!"

Clint stepped slowly from behind the raised desk. "Preacher, think on it some." Clint had spotted several deputies slipping up the front steps of the building. He hoped the boys didn't do nothing real sudden or foolish-like, 'cause he couldn't remember whether his pistol was even loaded; hadn't fired the damn thing in twenty years. Although he had certainly felt like shooting some citizens over the years.

The most exciting thing he'd seen the past ten years was when Old Lady Johnson had come to get her man out of the drunk tank and pulled a little pistol and started banging away. Shot her old man in the foot and damn near shot Sheriff Manville in the ass.

Then what Clint feared would happen . . . did. The young deputies just didn't know how to handle a bad situation.

One of them yelled out, "All of you men, freeze!"

Brother Edmund Reed spun around, the voice startling him, as it would most civilians. The muzzle of his rifle rose as he spun, as it usually would. The deputy shot him in the stomach and the .30-30 roared, the slug catching the deputy on the side of the face, taking off most of his jaw. The deputy died with a very curious expression on what was left of his young face.

Clint clawed for his sidearm, praying he could get it out in time; praying the damn thing was loaded; praying that he still could hit something with it. Through frantic, fearful eyes, the old dispatcher watched, as if in slow motion, the muzzle of Jack's shotgun come around and swing upward—toward him. He never heard the blast that tore his throat out, the double-ought slugs splattering blood and flesh all over the rear wall.

A dozen slugs from .357's and .38's and one .44 mag ripped into Jack Miller's body, flinging him back, slamming him to the floor, which, someone would discover while cleaning up the mess, was pink marble, covered with seventy years of grime. Jack's shotgun went off as it bounced on the floor, the slugs blasting through the open doors and hitting a woman driving by in a pickup. In the confusion of the bloody night, her body would not be discovered until morning.

"What in the hell is goin' on around here?" a deputy hollered. "The whole damn town is nuts!"

He would never know. For at that time, men and women stormed the jail and shot the deputies dead. They released the prisoners and set fire to the interior of the building. Another Anson creation was soon blazing in the night.

The music and the laughter in the Anson Hall was so loud that no one had heard the muffled explosion from the other end of town when the bank blew up. No one could call them, for the phone company building was dynamited, knocking out phones in that part of the county.

A member of Maxwell Anson's strikebreakers stepped outside for a breath of fresh air. The muzzle of a rifle suddenly propped up his chin. The man looked into the eyes of Adam Wallace.

"How many men in yonder?" Adam asked him. "And don't lie about it."

"I ain't gonna lie. Fifty-sixty, I guess. Man, please don't pull that trigger."

"That's up to you, Duke. You just walk over to that pickup with the camper on it and get your ass in back. Keep your hands in plain sight and don't do nothin' funny or jerky, you hear?"

"Loud and clear, Adam. I don't have no de-sire to die for a long time yet."

One of Anson's rednecks out of the way, Adam said, "Rosie, you got the men in position; all them townspeople set and ready?"

"Ready, Adam. We got the hall completely ringed."

Adam nodded his head. He lifted a bullhorn taken from Deputy Gardner's car to his lips. The electronically magnified voice was harsh and demanding in the night.

"You men in the Hall. Turn off that damned music and listen to me!"

The music was abruptly silenced. The night was quiet except for the faint popping and snapping of fires in town. A lone gunshot cut the stillness, but it was far away.

"What'd you want?" The question came from the Hall.

"You men got ten seconds to come out in single file, hands over your heads. No guns in sight. I'm counting, boys."

"Who you be out there?"

"Adam Wallace, and a hell of a lot of other people, all armed."

"Is that a fact?"

"Damn sure is!"

"What's 'at glow out 'air?"

"The bank buildin' and a couple of other Anson-owned places. All the prisoners were turned loose from the jail and the buildin' was set on fire. You boys beginnin' to get the message?"

"Come down to this, huh?"

"You got it."

"What happens if we don't come out?"

"We start shootin'."

There was a few seconds of silence from within the hall. Then a voice yelled, "Then let 'er rip, you sons a bitches!" A dozen shots rang out from the men inside the Hall. The men outside dived for cover.

Rapid gunfire split the night; muzzle blasts from rifles, shotguns, and pistols sparked and lanced in the damp darkness. Someone screamed in pain from inside the Hall. A man sank to his knees in the gravel parking lot. Blood poured from a hole in his belly. He screamed as the pain overcame shock and it rolled him to his side. Another slug struck him in the head. He died with his eyes open, staring at nothing.

The night rocked with gunfire and shouting and wild cursing.

The night of rage could not be contained until the fury had abated from the hearts and minds of all concerned.

Only death could tame it.

Barry chanced a look outside the room. The night was filled to overflowing with violence. He looked back at Brenda.

"You stay put. I'm going to walk the complex; take

a look around. I'll be right back. You have your pistol, don't hesitate to use it."

"Sounds like a war out there."

"It is. And it's going to get much worse before it's over. Fires have been set. Anson buildings, I'd bet."

"Good thing I don't have much money in the bank." Brenda tried to smile.

"I heard that. You stay put, now. I'll be right back."

Barry stepped out of the room, closing the door behind him. The sounds of gunfire was stronger; faint yelling drifted to him. He turned. Something smashed into the back of his head. He fell to his knees, not quite out. He could hear voices; Banger Anson's voice. It was faint. Then Barry pitched forward, blacking out as Brenda's screaming slowly faded into nothing and the darkness took him.

Sixteen

"What about him?" Hammer Kearn asked, pointing to Barry.

"Hell with him," Banger said. "Toss him in the room. Prissy pitcher-takin' queer." His eyes touched Brenda and he grinned. "Well, well, Miss Brenda. I tol' you time an' agin 'at someday I'd git to show you what I had to offer. And guess what? Tonight is the night. I'm gonna make you holler, baby."

The man is insane, she thought. *His whole world is collapsing around him and all he can think about is sex.*

"Don't do this, Banger." Anything to stall him. "The whole county is in revolt against you and your brothers and your father. Don't add more charges to those that will be brought against you. Think about it."

He grinned and rubbed his crotch. "Shit, baby!" He spat on the carpet. "We'll win this one jist lak we have all the rest. Don't you worry your purty little head over it. I got something that's gonna push all them thoughts plumb outta your brain-box."

"Let's get outta here, Banger," Hammer urged the man.

Brenda lunged for the door. Banger caught her easily. For a big man, he was very quick. He laughed at her struggling. She opened her mouth to scream, hoping some of the other lodgers might hear her; then she remembered they had been warned to stay in their rooms and not to come out for any reason.

Banger's hands roamed her body, squeezing and fondling.

"Hot damn!" he said. "She's ready for it, Hammer."

Hammer grunted. He was not interested in sex. He had already gotten his rocks off that evening. When he killed a man. "You be at the cabin?"

"Yeah. Just a humpin' Miss Brenda here. And her lovin' ever' minute of it."

Maxwell Anson knelt in the dirt beside the old warehouse and puked up his dinner, the hot bile spilling out of his mouth. He had never felt so disgusted with himself in all his adult life.

He had actually ejaculated in that child; and what made it even worse, he had enjoyed it. He might be past fifty, but the Anson magic was still working.

He gagged and vomited up what remained in his stomach. He felt a hot wetness on his cheeks and was not surprised to find tears streaming down his face.

But for what, and for whom, was the question that he could find no answer for.

The radio in Tay's unit was squawking its metallic, incomprehensible messages. Maxwell could not understand any of it so he tuned the silly garble out. He knelt there on the ground and wept; great gasping sobs. How ludicrous, he thought. I'm squatting here crying, and I'm lusting for the flesh of children.

He heard the door open behind him. His second son's voice.

"How come you got sick, Daddy?"

"Goddamn you!" Maxwell wiped his eyes. "Don't you know even that much?"

"Naw, sir. You just got you some mighty fine stuff in yonder, I figure. Way I see it, 'at ought to have made you feel purty good."

"Dear God in Heaven!" Maxwell rose to his feet. "What kind of people did I have a part in producing and what sort of genes did my father plant in me?"

A very faint inkling of what was wrong with his father managed to squirm its way into and through the murk of ignorance of what could be called Slapper's mental functionings. "Hale's faire, Daddy! We ain't—none of us—no more or no les' than what you allowed us to be-come. Surely you knowed what you was doin'. All them times you bought us out of trouble and stuff lak 'at. And they ain't no reason for you to feel bad 'bout takin' that little gal in yonder. We own this county; we got us a right to take what we want."

Maxwell shook his head. He did not believe that he was actually hearing the words from his son's mouth.

" 'Sides, Daddy, you've done a whole bunch of things in your life worser than rape. You—"

Maxwell looked at the bulk that was a part of his blood and flesh. "What the hell do you mean by that remark—uh?" He couldn't recall his son's Christian name. He knew he'd given him one, but what the hell was it?

The sounds of the girls' sobbing and pleading drifted out to the father and to the son. Only one noticed it.

His son's smile was arrogant and cruel and knowing

in the damp night. "Aw, hell, Daddy! This is me you talkin' to. You knowed Mine Number Twelve was bad when you sent them men in there seven-eight years ago. I recall you talkin' to the foreman. How many men died, Daddy? Ten, twelve? More? I don't 'member. And all them folks that wanted to join up and organize a union? McBane, Jamie Carlson, Charles Summers—and them four or five other men—oh, and don't forget that woman, Betty Wooden-hale. Daddy, you don't *really* think they just went away, do you?" His laugh was bitter in the night. "Banger kilt one. Ralph Causy arranged for Hammer Kearn to bust a cap on another. All us passed that woman around one night, then Eddie broke her neck and chunked her down a shaft. I beat old man Summers to death with a tar iron. Wilbur, he—"

Maxwell waved his son silent. He did not wish to hear more. For years he had managed to put all that—and a lot more evil—far back in his mind, deep in the recesses of no recall, far from the light of recognition. He sighed as the memories were dragged out into the light and he was forced to once more face them, to mentally taste the bitterness. He sighed and shook his head.

Slapper put his hand on his father's arm. "How old you, Daddy?"

"Fifty-eight . . ." He once more struggled to remember his son's Christian name. Finally, it came to him. "Hunter."

"For a man your age," Slapper grinned, "you done right well in yonder." He jerked his thumb toward the warehouse.

"What are you getting at, Hunter?"

"You Maxwell Anson, ain't you?"

"Of course, I am!"

"Well, you got judges and DA's in your pocket, don't you? You got people in federal office takin' Anson money, ain't you? There ain't nothin' gonna happen to none of us for tonight. I got it all figured out. When the town blew apart, we run out here and took cover. The bodies of them three girls in there ain't never gonna be found. Can't nothin' be proved on nobody. You see what I'm gettin' at, Daddy?"

It might just work, Maxwell thought. *It's so simple, we just might be able to pull it off.* Hell, it was worth a try.

Slapper was saying, "—so le's us just go back inside and let them in town kill each other."

The two men walked back into the warehouse. A few moments later, the screaming of the girls intensified.

"FBI!" Granger slid down on the gravel, showing Adam his I.D. He kept his head down as the lead whined and bounced and ricocheted around them. Slugs careening off the metal of cars and trucks sparked in the night. Deadly fireworks. The moaning of the wounded was a muted reminder that it was all real. The din was mind boggling.

Adam glanced at the I.D. and then spat out a brown stream of tobacco juice. "Wonderful," he said dryly. "Now why don't you just get out of the gawddamned way 'fore you get hurt." He pulled his .308 to his shoulder and blasted three quick rounds into the Hall.

"You don't understand." Granger had to shout to be heard. "I don't believe you are fully aware of the seriousness of this situation. Damn it, man, I am the FBI!"

"Big deal," Adam remarked. "You put your britches on one leg at a time, don't you?"

"What?"

"That badge don't mean jack crap to me."

He reloaded his rifle.

Granger looked at him in amazement. This was not working out the way it usually did. What was the matter with these people? People were supposed to show respect for the office—for the Bureau.

"This has got to stop!" Granger said.

"No way, partner. Not till all them bastards in there is dead!"

"My God, man! Do you want to be charged with murder?"

"Don't make a shit to me. Be your word against several hundred. I'd think about that, was I you."

Granger thought about it. With a sigh, he said, "I would like to talk to the men inside the Hall."

"Your option." Adam once more began banging away at the building.

When he had exhausted the clip, Granger picked up the bullhorn Adam had used and shouted down the shooting. "FBI!" he informed the men. "You in the Hall. Drop your weapons and come on out. I'll guarantee your safety."

"In a pig's ass!" the shout was returned. "How in the hell are you gonna do that? How many of you is there?"

Granger hesitated. He wanted this war stopped, but wanted also to tell the truth; give the men in the building a chance to come out of this mess alive. "Just me."

The men in the Hall laughed, their derisive laughter harsh. "Shore, Granger. Shore you'll protect us. I got me a pitcher of that."

"Damn!" Granger said. He lifted the bullhorn to his lips, hesitated for a few seconds. "I know you have women in there with you. How about asking them if they'd like to get clear?"

"They'll just run," Adam said.

"Stay out of this."

"Yes, sir. Mister FBI-man."

"That's a truth," the spokesman called from the building. "All right. We'd be obliged if you'd let them get gone. They ain't fired on nobody; ain't got nothin' to do with this quarrel."

Adam snorted mockingly.

"OK to let the women leave?" Granger asked Adam.

"Them bitches in there is just as bad as the men. Or worse. But—yeah, hell, I'll hold my fire. But I ain't gonna speak for nobody else out here."

Granger looked around him. The men he could see were nodding their heads in agreement. Using the bullhorn, he asked the others to hold their fire; let the women get clear. After a few seconds, the firing ceased. "You women in the Hall! Come on out and get clear."

"We gittin' in our trucks and pullin' out!" a woman called, her voice shrill. "And we're armed, by God. So don't none of you trash try to stop us."

"Erin Ramsey," Adam spat out the words. "That is one sorry slut if there ever was one. I'll bet you she'll be dead 'fore this is all over."

Granger wasn't about to take any bets on that. "Everybody hold their fire!" Granger shouted through the bullhorn, the words echoing around the area. "All right, ladies—"

Adam got a good laugh out of that.

"Come on out. You're cleared to leave."

A dozen women ran from the building, using a side door. They split up. Granger recognized most of them, including Jennifer and Jane. They jumped into cars and trucks and roared away.

"Now what?" Granger asked. The silence was so strange it was almost unnerving after the roar and boom of gunfire.

A man in the Hall carelessly exposed an arm in a window. A shot split the night. The man screamed and fell away.

"That," Adam said.

Granger fell to the gravel as the night once more vented its rage.

"Strip," Banger told her. "And do it nice and slow-like. I been waitin' a long time for this here show. I wanna enjoy it."

"I will not!"

Banger slapped her, the open-handed blow almost knocking Brenda off her feet. She staggered back, putting out a hand, grabbing the edge of a sofa. She tasted blood in her mouth.

"I can make it a lot rougher for you, baby," Banger said. "And you damn well better believe that. So if you're into pain, I can shore provide a bunch of it for you." He unbuckled his belt and slid it out of the loops, wrapping it once around his hand, letting the leather dangle. "You like pain, baby?"

"No." It was said quickly but quietly.

"Then strip!"

She nodded, her fingers working at the buttons. Her head began to clear. A small trickle of blood oozed out one corner of her mouth.

Banger licked his lips when she was naked from the waist up, blouse and bra on the floor.

"Come over here, bitch!"

She walked to where he was sitting in a straight-backed chair. She silently endured his hands on her.

"Nice," Banger said. "Soft and smooth, just lak I always knowed it would be. Now peel outta them jeans and show me the rest."

Barry groaned and got to his knees, then to his feet, trying to determine where he was and what had happened to him.

He looked around the dark room. Brenda's quarters. He found the light switch and flooded the room with light, but only after banging his shin on a coffee table. His head throbbed with pain. He felt for blood. None. Just a lump on the back of his head. He washed his face with cold water and took several aspirin.

Brenda was gone, of course. But now was not the time for the luxury of panic. Had to think things out rationally.

He cautiously opened the door to her quarters and looked outside, all senses working at full capacity. He could detect no one near. He stepped out as the sounds of gunfire reached his ears. Walking to his trailer, he transferred explosives to the Kenworth.

Barry checked his weapons, fully loaded.

Then something came drifting out of his brain;

something he'd heard just before slipping into darkness after he was struck.

Banger's name.

All right. That's something. He let his truck warm up, sitting behind the wheel, thinking.

He almost shot out of reflex as someone struck the side of his tractor. He looked out the window.

A woman, dressed in nightclothes. "I'm scared half out of my mind, mister," she said. "Me and my husband just stopped here to spend the night. I don't know what's going on. But I saw two men drag a woman out of her room. They said something about going to one of their cabins."

"Thank you, ma'am. Go back to your room and stay inside. You haven't seen anything; you don't know anything. Let the cops handle it. OK?"

"Damn well betcha!"

She ran across the concrete and back into her room.

Barry would bet on Banger's cabin. But where the hell was it?

He put the Kenworth in gear and pulled out. One way to find out. Ask somebody.

He stopped and questioned three people before he could find one that didn't run at the sight of him.

"North. Go past the crossroads. The cabin is set off the road; be to your right. When you get there, mister, do me a favor?"

"What's that?"

"Kill the son of a bitch for me!"

Willie Jefferson thought he had never in his life experienced such awful pain. Not even when he had been wounded in the war. His stomach was badly swollen, blood from his ruptured spleen pushing to be free. Every movement was agony; every breath a lancing, searing hot pain jabbing at him through his cracked and broken ribs. He was coughing up a lot of pinkish foam; knew a lung was punctured. He fought to stay conscious; he was so very weary. Wanted to go to sleep but knew if he did, he would never awaken. And he had something very important to do before he allowed himself the luxury of that pain-free eternal sleep.

A car came into view. No, a truck, parked by the side of the road. Lucas's old pickup. Willie pulled off the road and painfully made his way on foot to the truck. He looked inside. Empty.

Lightning illuminated the grounds. Willie spotted something in the ditch. A jacket. Then his eyes found the man he had called friend since grade school days.

"Aw, Lucas," he whispered. "Look like you didn't even get to fire a shot for what you believed in. I'm sorry, old friend."

Lucas's hands were by his side. He was kneeling, facedown, in a meadow. He had been shot in the back of the head, the impact swelling his head. Willie could see the exit hole, just above the eye.

"It's happenin', Lucas. Come mornin', there ain't nothin' gonna be left of the Ansons' evil. Bet on it. And if I can get some in gunsights, it won't take till morning."

The winds picked up, sighing mournfully across the meadow in the night.

Willie looked down at his friend. "I'll see you 'fore long, friend. Then we can just sit and talk and live in peace."

Willie recalled, through his pain, a shortcut to town. He turned down a gravel road. It would take him past an old Anson warehouse.

He was not aware of the car following him, staying some distance back, traveling without lights. The car had three men in it.

Hard-eyed, heavily armed, grim-faced men. One of them was looking for his nieces.

Brenda felt dirty and soiled, although the cabin was clean and neat and Banger had taken her to bed to culminate his assault. He had threatened to torture her if she offered any further resistance. She had endured the rape. She lay quietly, not wanting to make him angry; that he was unstable was quite obvious to her.

"Come on, baby!" he urged. "Let's do it again."

"I don't want to."

"Well, now, Brenda baby, it don't make a bit of difference what you want or don't want." He told her what would happen if she didn't roll over and cooperate.

She rolled over on her back, looking up at the ceiling, hate making her eyes bright.

She did not take her eyes from the ceiling as he raped her again. She detached her mind from her body and spent the next ten minutes recalling the words to songs that had been popular when she was in high school.

He cursed her when she would not allow him to kiss her.

She endured the indignity.

* * *

Gritting his teeth in rage, Barry was driving too fast and he knew it, sliding around curves, kicking up gravel, fishtailing the rear end. The stacks were boiling out diesel smoke.

He caught a glimpse of lights from a house set well back from the road, in a stand of timber. He shifted down and backed up, cutting his lights and pulling into the drive. He jumped from the truck and ran to the cabin. Looking in a window, he cursed under his breath.

The naked bulk of Banger was covering Brenda. Barry ran to the front porch, took the steps two at a time, and tried the doorknob. It turned under his hand. He pushed open the door.

"We gotta do something!" Niven Simmons told his partner. "Damn it, we can't just sit back and watch them folks burn down the damn town."

His partner, Sergeant Peter Mills, looked at him. A long look of amazement. "You went to college for five years and that's the best you can come up with?"

The men lay under the partial protection of a stand of trees on a hill overlooking Anson.

Peter said, "I think you must have took a lick up side your head, boy! You sure you feel all right? Man, there mus' be four-five hundred people down there; all of 'em got a gun of some sort—even the women! We can't get close enough to use our handy-talkies. We can't get out; the roads is blocked. So what would you have us do? Jump right up in the big fat middle of it all and wave our magic badges, hollerin', 'All right now, folks, this is the State Po-lice, all both of us. Y'all cease and desist, now, you hear?' Shit, Niven—you plumb out of your mind, boy!"

Niven spat a stream of tobacco juice, nailing a cricket in the middle of a chirp. "Well, hell, Pete, we cain't just lay up here and watch them folks carry on like a bunch of heathens."

"I'd lak to know just what in the hell is gonna prevent me from doin' just that?"

Both men were well remembered at the University of Kentucky for possessing the dubious distinction of being able to almost completely destroy the English language and still graduate in the top ten of their class. Three point seven grade average. And as Niven had said, "Out of four, that's right good, ain't it?"

" 'Cause we're lawmen, that's why we gotta do something."

"You right there, boy. But do I have to remind you that we is *live* lawmen? We go down there"—he pointed toward the smoky town—"and we gonna be *dead* lawmen!"

"You do have a point."

"Bet your ass, I do."

"Wonder how that FBI feller is doin'?"

"Well—the hell with all of you, then!" Granger shouted, his voice not carrying ten feet over the roar of gunfire. "I'll see to it that you're all brought up on charges. I'll see to it that you're all tried in a court of law. Every one of you. And that's a promise. And I mean to keep it, too."

He paused for breath, looking around him. Nobody was paying the slightest bit of attention to him. He felt like a fool.

"Aw, hell, Granger," Adam said to him. They both were squatting behind a truck. "Why don't you just shut up?"

The FBI agent grabbed the miner by his shirtfront and shook him. "Adam, why can't you get it through your head that I am an FBI agent? A federal officer—and I am ordering you and your people to lay down your guns and stand easy until I can get more people in here to restore order."

Adam balled his right hand into a fist and shook it under Granger's nose. "If you don't turn me a-loose, boy, I'm gonna knock the pure-dee piss slap outta you."

Granger released him.

"Thank you much."

"You're welcome," Granger replied wearily. "Well, to hell with it! I don't give a damn if you all get killed. Crazy bunch of hardheaded hillbillies!"

Adam grinned at him. "But you one too, boy."

Granger looked at him without replying. He shook his head and retreated back to his unit, crawling part of the way to avoid the gunfire. He cranked up and drove away from the scene of fighting.

The entire town of Anson, or so it seemed, was a battleground, with pockets of Anson haters doing battle with pockets of Anson supporters. Granger skirted the heavier fighting and once more looked at his radio. It was still smashed. Wouldn't have done much good anyway. The mountains would prevent most transmissions from getting very far.

They were cut off.

Granger concluded that there was nothing he could do. Then he recalled the high ground overlooking the town square. He drove up there, parked, and got out, standing in the mist, looking down at the flashes of gunfire and the fools behind the guns, shooting at other fools.

No, he thought, sighing. *They are not fools; the law failed them, that's all.*

"And who might you be, Deputy?" The voice came out at him from under a tree.

Granger spun, one hand on the butt of his pistol.

"Whoa, boy!" the voice said. "Take 'er easy, now. If you friendly, so are we."

"I'm Special Agent Granger Kildare, Federal Bureau of Investigation. I've been working undercover in this area for months. Now, who are you?"

"I'm Sergeant Niven Simmons and this here feller to my left is Sergeant Peter Mills. Kentucky State Police."

"I knew you weren't flatlanders. Nobody can fake that accent."

"I do believe I de-tect Kentucky in you, too, Mister FBI person."

"You betcha." Granger laughed sourly. "Well, for all our badges and training, we're sure doing a lot of law enforcement this night, aren't we?"

"Stayin' alive is what we're doin'. Kind of brings to mind what that feller said about discretion and bravery, don't it?"

"For a fact. Y'all mind if I join you?"

"Sit 'er squat. Either way, you gonna get your ass wet."

Seventeen

Barry jerked Banger off the woman, in his rage, flinging the naked man all the way across the room, to land in a sprawl by the fireplace. Barry tossed his pistol on the bed and moved toward the oldest Anson whelp. He wanted this to be with fists and boots. He was going to make sure Banger Anson never raped another woman.

Banger cursed him, jumping to his feet, roaring his rage like a maddened bull. He grabbed a poker and closed with Barry, swinging the poker viciously, the iron whistling through the air. Barry ducked and stepped in close, kicking out, his boot catching Banger on the bare kneecap. The bully howled in pain and dropped the poker, which clattered to the floor.

Barry stepped in closer and drove his right fist into Banger's soft belly, driving the breath from him with a whooshing sound. He brought his left hand around, knife edge of the hand up, and delivered a vicious chop to the side of Banger's neck.

Banger fell backward and stumbled across the room, shaking his head, gathering strength and wind.

He tried to box Barry and Barry took a hard right to his head. It stung, but not enough to dispel the rage within the man.

Barry slammed a left and a right to the man's jaw, knocking the man back, bloodying his mouth. Banger tried to grab Barry in a bear hug, to break his ribs or back with his enormous strength. Barry kicked him in the groin.

Screaming, puke running down his chin, Banger dropped to his knees.

Barry kicked the man in the face with a boot, snapping Banger's head back. Teeth rolled and clicked on the hardwood floor as Banger screamed in pain, blood from his smashed lips and gums spraying the air.

And then, with a coolness filling him and with methodical deadliness, Barry proceeded to kick Banger's face apart. Barry then kicked the man's penis and ball sac up into his belly. Banger had long since passed out from the pain. He would never again rape anybody.

A pistol shot spun Barry around, his chest heaving from his exertions. A dark-complexioned man was slowly sinking to the threshold of the open front door. There was a hole in the center of his head. Brenda stood by the bed, weeping, naked, holding Barry's pistol with both hands.

"Hammer Kearn," she said, her voice breaking from emotion. Her eyes were closed. "I don't want to look at him. You tell me. Did I hit him?"

Barry smiled. "You sure did. Right between the eyes."

She opened her eyes and looked. "Damn!"

"What's the matter?"

"I was aiming at his stomach."

The pain was so fierce Willie had to pull off the road, the car behind him doing the same. Willie still had not spotted the car. With each breath, the black man was spitting up gobs of blood. He knew a rib was sticking through a lung; his stomach was swelling more and more with blood. He rested for a moment, then raised his head from the steering wheel and looked at a faint glow of lights off to his left.

He thought he heard the sound of laughter. Party laughter, full of drunkenness. He thought he must be dreaming, for he knew there were no houses along this stretch of back road. Then he remembered the old Anson warehouse.

"That's funny," he muttered. "That place's been shut down for years." He started to drive on; then he heard someone scream in pain. A woman's voice. No, a girl's voice. His face hardened. "Check this out." He turned off the engine and lights and slowly, painfully, got out, pulling his rifle with him.

Behind him, unseen by Willie, on the same side of the road as the warehouse, three men were running silently, swiftly toward the building. They carried short-barreled weapons.

Willie slowly hobbled up the gravel, each staggering step agony for the man. As he drew nearer, he could hear more screaming. Different screaming. *More than one woman or girl in that place,* he thought. The girls were screaming in pain with degradation.

"Oh, sweet Jesus!" Willie muttered. He remembered his own Lisa Mae's wailing.

He tried to hurry. He soon gave that up as the pain became too much for him to bear. He relegated himself to a hobbling walk. As he turned up the weed-filled old driveway, the front door opened and Tay Blessing stepped out, naked from the waist down. He looked rather stupid in his boots.

The sounds of screaming were much louder now. Not a word, but more a single, unwavering note of agony. The note drifted to Willie, grating on his brain. Enraging him.

"Y'all save me some of that blond-headed gal," Tay called over his shoulder. "Soon as I whiz I want some more. I like to hear her holler."

A screaming plea was shoving painfully into the night.

"Redneck white-trash filth!" Willie said. He threw the rifle to his shoulder and centered the iron sights on Blessing's lower belly and pulled the trigger.

The man's right wrist disintegrated and was driven into his belly by the heavy slug. Blessing's howlings were rich in the steamy night.

Deputy Jerry Ryan filled the doorway. He was stark naked, a pistol in his hand. Willie shot him in the chest as his own blood filled his mouth and nose. Willie slowly sank to his knees, dying. He did not hear the slug that slammed into his chest; did not hear or feel the second shot that tore into his neck; did not hear the men gathering around him; and did not understand their confusion as he said, "Hi, Lucas. Tol' you I'd see you soon."

"Who the hell is he talkin' to?" Slapper asked.

"He ain't talkin' to nobody, man. Hell, he's dead!"

"So are you." The voice came from behind the knot of naked and near-naked men.

Slapper and his buddies turned to see three men standing by the warehouse. They were shrouded in darkness. But the rednecks could see they held funny-looking weapons in their hands. Pointing at them.

"Where'd you boys come from?" Whacker asked.

The three men laughed grimly. The tall one said, "The Promised Land."

"Haw?" Slapper asked.

"Are you an Anson?"

"Yeah. And so's he." Slapper jerked a thumb toward Whacker.

"How nice for both of you," Colonel Wiseman spoke.

The three of them did not see the two men slip out the back door of the warehouse, running for the timber.

"My brother, Sol, sends his wishes for your early demise," the tall man said.

"Sol . . . Wiseman?" Whacker asked, a feeling of pure fear filling him.

"That is correct, you pig!"

"Now whut?" Slapper mouthed. He was too stupid to know what was going on.

"Now . . . shalom," the tall man said.

"Whut kind of shit is that?"

"Well, translating it into a vernacular that even the most ignorant can comprehend, it means, 'Adios, motherfuckers'!"

The Uzi's began chanting Old Testament scriptures.

Barry drove Brenda back to town, passing by the besieged Anson Hall. Leaving her in the truck, with orders to keep her head down, he slipped through the maze of vehicles and gunfire until he found Adam.

"Adam, I have a case of grenades, two M-10's, couple thousand rounds of ammo, and a sack full of C-4. You know what I'm talking about?"

"I was Marine Force Recon, Mister Rivera." He answered a lot of questions with just that.

"They're in my truck."

"Henry!" Adam yelled. "You and Paul get that gear outta Mister Rivera's truck. You'll know what it is when you see it. Don't ask no questions; just bring it here."

"Would you also have someone take Brenda to the hospital over the county line?"

Adam barked out those orders, then swung his gaze back to Barry, his eyes filled with unasked questions.

Barry answered many of them simply. "Banger will be a long time recovering. I stomped his face in and kicked his balls into his belly—"

Adam lifted one eyebrow.

"Literally. He's ruined as a man. He's at a cabin 'bout ten miles from town."

"Set back off the road a piece, back up in the timber?"

"Yes."

"I know where it is. I'll have someone fetch the bastard."

"Yes. Because I want him to live."

"Yeah," Adam grinned. "The doc might have to amputate."

"That is a distinct possibility. And I want him to go to prison without any equipment."

"Mister Barry Rivera, I don't never want you for an enemy."

"It'll never happen, Adam. We'll probably never see one another again."

"I figured that when you asked me to send someone else with Brenda. You're pullin' out, then?"

"Let's just say it would probably be best if I did not

have to make any official statements concerning this matter."

Adam grinned and stuck out his hand. "Sure has been a pleasure knowin' you, Mister Rivera. A real pleasure."

Barry shook the hand. "Take care of Brenda, Adam. She is a truly nice person."

"I'll do it personal."

Barry slipped away into the night.

The explosives and weapons were placed beside Adam. "All right, boys. Now let's give them Anson-lovin' bastards what-for."

The first series of explosions brought the two Kentucky State cops and the FBI agent leaping to their feet, running to the edge of the hill.

"Holy jumpin' Jesus and Mary!" Niven said. "What's goin' on down there now?"

"That wasn't dynamite," Pete said. "Sounded more like grenades. Kind of whump-thumpin' sound to me."

The tat-a-tat-a-tat of rapid-fire weapons brought them to silence on the hill.

"Submachine guns," Granger said glumly. "Sounded like MAC's to me. I wonder where Adam got them?"

"How do you know it's this Adam that's got them?" Niven asked.

Barry Rivera leaped into Granger's brain. "That is something to think about."

A violent explosion rocked the night. Flames began leaping into the dark misty sky. The screaming of mortally wounded men could be heard.

"Shi-ittt!" Pete drawled. "That might have been some dynamite, but I handled C-4 before. And if I was a bettin' man . . ." He let that trail off into silent speculation.

Niven looked at Granger. "Radio in your sheriff's unit workin'?"

"Smashed. It's hell gettin' out of these mountains even when it is workin'."

"Dandy."

"How'd y'all get here?"

"Pickup truck. Thought we was gonna have a little more time than it turned out we did."

Granger thought for a moment on the grammatical content of that statement. He shook his head. "Radio?"

"Not none to speak of. CB."

"Range?"

"When we cut in that booster, it'll do some talkin', now. What're you thinkin'?"

"Let's see if we can't find a way out of here. Get close enough to Ellen County to get in touch with Son Cody's men. They can relay for us."

"Worth a try," Pete said. "Let's do it." He pointed toward the now-burning Hall. "It's fixin' to get gamey down yonder."

Ralph Causy answered the hammering on his front door. He stood for a few seconds in shock. Maxwell Anson stood on the porch. The man was soaking wet, his clothing muddy and torn, his hair disheveled. Ralph waved his employer inside.

"Maxwell! The entire town has gone nuts. What in the name of God happened to you?"

"No time for explanations. Start destroying any papers you might have here. When that is done, get to your office and do the same. Then get on the horn and start transferring funds to our South American operations. Have the monies ready to be transferred when the banks in New York open. Then destroy the books—everything. Set the damn place on fire. Way those trashy bastards outside are behaving, we can blame it all on them. Have you seen the girls?"

"No. They went to the Hall this afternoon."

"Fucking right up to when their world falls around them. Hell with them. Look, take your car; I'll use your pickup. We've got to make plans to get the hell gone at first light."

"We!"

"Damn right . . . we! You're up to your ass in this just as I am. I'd think about that if I were you, Ralph."

Ralph did. Quickly. "See your point. Where are the boys? Your boys?"

"Eddie's runnin' scared. We got split up. I know two of them are dead."

"Dead!" Ralph's friend had relayed the news with absolutely no sign of emotion.

"Yeah. Out at the old warehouse. Three men with machine guns popped up . . . ah! Hell with it. Move, Ralph. I don't know how much time we have left."

Barry looked up and pulled out of the motel parking area. Most of the roads were open, the men who had manned the blockades now fighting in town. Barry rolled a few miles out of town and parked, listening to the chatter on his CB.

He heard Eddie's voice, excited, speaking to his brother, Bugger.

"Got to git gone from here, boy. Hit's all comin' apart. Daddy done run off and lef' us for the dogs, and the hounds is closin' in fas'."

"Where's Slapper and Whacker?"

"Dead. Soldier boys from the Jew army kilt them both—and some others, too."

"How the hell did they git involved?"

"Don't know. What's your twenty?"

" 'Bout two mile east of town. Climbin' up Misty Mountain."

Barry's location.

"Hale's faire! I'm raight behind you. I see your tail lights."

Barry pulled out and backed up, pointing the nose of his Kenworth back down the hill. He rolled forward, staying right in the middle of the winding highway.

He would know the Anson trucks; they had enough lights on them to light up a small city. He smiled a grim warrior's smile.

The hound was indeed closing in. "Call me Dog," he muttered, picking up speed.

He could see the redneck pickups coming up the mountain, fast. He picked up his CB mic. "Anson trash. You hear me."

"Who you callin' trash, boy!" his speaker crackled.

"You, you ignorant bastards!"

"You better watch your mouth, boy! Who you be, anyways?"

"Dog."

"Hit's that crazy man been sparkin' Miss Brenda!" Eddie hollered. "He be comin' down the mountain. See his lights yonder?"

"I see 'em. Break it off, you fool! You'll run us off the road!"

"That is my intention, rednecks."

"I'm gone, Eddie!" Bugger hollered. "You bes' turn around if you can."

Barry could see the pickup slew around in the road and head back down the mountain. Bugger's pickup was coming up fast.

The last thing Bugger would remember, as he went hurtling off the road and sailing out into open space, falling, falling, were the lights of the Kenworth he had tried to avoid and a man called Dog cursing him on the CB.

Then Barry was roaring down the mountain, right on the back end of Eddie's pickup.

"You git away from me!" Eddie screamed into his mic. "You crazy bassard!"

Barry rammed him.

"That's for all the little girls you've ruined over the years, you asshole," Barry told him.

"I be sorry for all that," Eddie squalled. "I be good from now on. I promise you I will."

Barry rammed him again, the pickup slewing from side to side.

The pickup rolled over on its side and went shrieking down the road, sparking with the terrible sounds of metal grinding loud in the night. Eddie was flung out. Barry ran over him.

"One less redneck in the world," he muttered.

And kept on trucking.

The Anson family's decades'-old evil hold on the area was almost broken; only a few minor loose ends had to be tied up neatly and knotted.

When the roof of the Anson Hall was blown into

flaming debris by the grenades and the C-4, those inside who were not seriously hurt were taken to the local gym where they were placed under guard until someone could figure out what to do with them.

"Shoot them," was one suggestion.

"Probably be better off if we did," Adam said. "But I guess we'd better not."

"Aw, shit, Adam!"

Adam shifted his base of operations to the courthouse, where Jud Manville and his few remaining deputies had barricaded themselves in.

"Where's Goldie, Manville?" Adam yelled through the bullhorn. He knew in his guts, but wanted to hear it from Jud.

A rifle shot came from the courthouse, followed by, "You're all under arrest, Wallace."

Hooting laughter echoed around the outside of the building. "Why don't you come out here and put the cuffs on me, Manville?" Adam yelled.

He turned to a man. "Van, work in close and lob one of those grenades in through a window. Be sure it's HE and not WP; we don't wanna burn the place slap down. One of those HE's should get their attention right well."

It definitely got their attention. One of the deputies who had tortured Goldie was standing by the window in the darkened room when the grenade smashed through, bouncing along the floor. It spread him all over the room, blew out all the windows, and caused Jud Manville to dirty his underwear.

When the smoke and dust had settled, Adam lifted the bullhorn. "One more time, Manville—where is Goldie and the girls?"

"Jesus Christ!" Jud screamed, shaking his pants legs. "You've killed Pittman. Adam! Stop it. Goldie's dead."

Adam turned to look into the eyes of Granger Kildare. The FBI man had slipped quietly up behind him. "You hearin' all this, Granger?"

"Yes. Go ahead with your questioning, Adam. All this is so legally fucked up, one more fuck-up won't matter."

Adam lifted the bullhorn. "How did he die, Jud?"

"We—ah, got a little careless with a cattle prod." *Hell,* the man thought, *might as well level with them. Might keep me from getting strung up to the nearest tree limb.*

"Sure, it was an accident," Adam said, just loud enough for Granger to hear. "Just like all those other men and women who've been tortured and sodomized and raped and killed in the jail—among other places, that is."

"We know," Granger said. "We've been working on this for a long time. Just waiting to get the whole bunch of them."

"Damn sure took you guys long enough." Adam's tone was bitter and accusing. "What the hell was you waitin' on?"

"To do it legally."

"Piss on legal, Granger. That's what's wrong with this country now. Every 'i' has to be dotted. "Every 't' crossed. Or some fuckin' lawyer will get it tossed out. You wanna argue with that?"

"Off the record?"

"Hell, yes."

"No. I can't argue with it."

"How can you work the way you do? Seein' innocent

people done like the Ansons done folks, and not wantin' to just kill them?"

With a sigh, the FBI man said, "We do want to kill at times, Adam. Believe me."

Adam smiled. "I knew you was one of us hill folks. Fancy degree and a hotshot federal badge can't do nothin' but step aside when generations come callin' out of the past."

"That's . . . an interesting way of putting it, Adam. Now listen to me. I want this ended. Right now. We both know there was someone in here who's killed this night. No names. Now, I just spoke with Goldie's sister-in-law. She's in bad shape. She was with Ruth and Esther Wiseman out at the old warehouse. They were all three very badly used. We know that two of the Anson boys are dead—Slapper and Whacker. Don't know where Eddie and Bugger got off. Maxwell was part of the rape. He's at his house; men from the State Police have sealed it off. He's not going anywhere. Jerry and Tay Blessing are dead. Willie Jefferson shot them. We've got it sewed up, Adam; we're taking statements now. Son Cody and people are coming in, along with a contingent of State Police. It's over, Adam."

Adam handed the MAC-10 to Granger. Granger took it with a sigh of relief. Adam said, "Off the record?"

"Yes. You have my word."

"Banger kidnapped Brenda. Took her out to his cabin. Raped her. That truck driver fellow stomped him pretty good—so I heard. Ugly son of a bitch to begin with; no tellin' what he'll look like now. He's still out there. Brenda kilt Hammer Kearn."

Granger nodded his head at the information. A

man walked up to him and said, "Granger, I just come in from my place; seen Lucas Webster's old truck parked alongside the road. Got out and looked around. Found the preacher in a meadow. Somebody shot him in the back of the head. He's dead."

"Thank you, sir."

"Welcome." The man walked off into the night.

"I lost about half a dozen people myself," Adam said. "Another ten-twelve shot up. Deputy Gardner's locked up out in the country. I'll go get him. He's got a lick up side the head, but that's all."

"Thank you, Adam. Tell your people to go home and don't leave the county until we talk with them. But for now, its over."

It was only minutes from breaking dawn. A misty dawn in Dane County. Smoke hung low over the valley.

But Granger had been wrong.

It was not yet over.

Eighteen

The woman stood impassively, watching her husband hurriedly throw articles of clothing into suitcases. She shook her head and said, "I'm not going with you, Charlie. I mean that."

"Then stay here and be damned!" Mayor Bradley said. "I'm not going to prison."

"They'll catch you," she warned him. "And then it'll be only worse than if you'd stayed and faced whatever charges you think they'll have against you."

"They might catch me. But I got money squirreled away that you don't know nothin' about. They'll have themselves a good hard run comin' after me."

His wife turned her back to him and walked out of the bedroom into the den. Charlie heard her gasp of shock and quickly followed her. He stopped dead in his tracks, his heartbeat picking up and his skin turning clammy with cold sweat. Johnny Springer stood in the den, a pistol in his hand. He was bloody; pink froth bubbled from his lips. He had been shot several times, one of the slugs hitting a lung, the other slug hitting him in the stomach. He was walking around, dying.

"Come to pay you . . . a visit," Johnny wheezed the

words. "Pay you back . . . for what you done to my . . . little girl. You sorry . . . bastard."

"What do you mean, Johnny?" the woman asked. "What did my husband do to your little girl?" Full knowledge of her husband's rumored past flooded her mind. She had heard the whispered talk for years; had chosen to ignore it. Charlie had such a good position in the community, and being mayor for years meant one rubbed elbows with the right people. Including the Anson family. "Oh, no, Johnny! Not the girl who was raped?"

"Yes'um. Your man there . . ." He coughed up blood. "And the Anson boys . . . took her and raped her. Said . . . it was one way of me . . . payin' my debts to them. But first they stomped me. And then they . . . made me watch. Your man then . . . had his fun with me while I was down and bloody."

The wife turned horror-filled eyes toward her husband. "Yes. And I can just imagine what it was, too."

"He's lying!" Bradley screamed.

"No," his wife said, a weariness in her voice. "No, he's not lying."

She turned and walked into the kitchen, poured a cup of freshly brewed coffee. She sat down at the table and waited for the tears to come. But they would not. She could feel only contempt for her husband, and, she admitted, foul cheapness for herself. She had kept her head buried in the sand for too many years. As so many others had done, she had known what was happening in Dane County, but had chosen to remain silent and wear blinders.

She jumped as the pistol blasted the silence. She heard a thump, like a heavy body hitting the floor. Then another thump followed the first one.

She stood up and took her coffee to the back porch, sitting down in an old rocker. Just breaking light in the east. Be a while till the sun broke free of the mountains. But it would be a pretty day, she reckoned. The rain was gone. Might work out in the yard. Do some much-needed pruning. Never could get her husband to do much around the house or yard.

Then she started crying.

But she didn't know why or for whom.

Ralph Causy was just turning on the shredder when a voice spoke from the darkened hall of the Anson Office Building.

"I wouldn't do that, sir."

Ralph looked up. Granger Kildare. But he was not wearing his deputy's clothing. He was dressed in a neat business suit. Some kind of I.D. pinned to the breast pocket of the jacket. He also had a gun in his hand. Pointed at Ralph.

"Why is that, Granger? And why are you pointing that weapon at me?"

"We need those papers for evidence, to answer your first question. The answer to your second question is that I might have to shoot you."

"Well, I certainly hope it will not come to that. You say 'we'?"

"Federal Bureau of Investigation."

"How interesting." Causy turned off the paper shredder and sat down behind his desk. He rubbed his face and sighed wearily. "Tell you the truth, I'm glad it's over. I really am. It is over, isn't it?"

"Just about, sir. Now I must advise you that you have the right to remain silent—"

"Oh, hell, Kildare! I'm an attorney. I know all that."

"If you give up that right, anything you say can be used against you in a court of law—"

"Granger!" Causy said impatiently.

"You have a right to speak with an attorney. If you cannot afford one, an attorney will be appointed. Do you understand your rights?"

"Yes, Granger." He laughed. "It's past time for it to end. Should never have started. I will give you people my full cooperation in exchange for, ah, certain concessions on your part."

"I'll keep that in mind."

"Have you seen my daughter?"

"No, sir. Stand up, turn around, and put your hands flat against the wall. Spread your feet, please."

Causy did as ordered. "This is very humiliating, you know. I'm glad no one is around to see this."

Granger thought of the weeping and violated girls he had seen from the warehouse. The tortured body of Goldie. The dead littering the valley.

And this bastard thinks his arrest is humiliating. Granger almost shot him.

Tate didn't go with the men who came to tell him that his daddy was dead. Tate knew what dead meant. He watched the men leave as he sat on the old front porch. He sat for a long time. Dawn had busted free and clear, lighting everything. It was Tate's favorite time of the day. Everything was so pretty and fresh. He watched as the pickup truck pulled into the driveway.

Two white ladies. Miss Jane and Miss Jenny. Tate

had finally worked things out in his mind that they had been a part of his daddy's dying.

He rose from the porch and walked toward the truck and the two grinning, evil women. Tate had a surprise for them. But he didn't think it was gonna be no fun surprise.

"And there was no looting at all?" Sheriff Son Cody asked Granger.

The streets of Anson were now patrolled with heavily armed deputies from other counties and by equally heavily armed State Police.

"Not one incident we can find," Granger replied. "The only buildings burned belonged to the Anson family."

Son Cody still had not gotten over his men finding that near-hysterical redneck handcuffed to the roll bar of the hot rod. He told Granger about it.

"And he says a truck driver killed the men at the garage and smashed the building?"

The sheriff nodded.

"Probably lying. I haven't seen any new faces driving rigs. Just that Toby fellow."

"I've got men inspecting the shaft the bodies were tossed down. They report lots of human bones there. And they found Toby Kendall's body."

Granger nodded.

Son looked around him. "A lot of hate," he observed. "Years of it. Knew it had to come."

"Yes."

"Those MAC-10's?"

"Sterile weapons," Granger told him. "No way to trace them."

"Where'd the men get them?"

Granger laughed. "Sheriff, nobody seems to know anything about anything. Everybody has an alibi."

"It's going to be a mess charging people, isn't it?"

"That is putting it mildly."

Son said, "OK, let's count it down. Slapper and Whacker are dead. Reports are that three men from the Israeli Army killed them. Seems to me like somebody could come up with a better story than that, doesn't it to you?"

"Seems that way."

"Israel Army!" Son shook his head. "Well, Banger looks like he might live. But his, ah, equipment is shot. All he can do about sex now is dream of how it used to be. The dead include Blessing—and that is a blessing—Bradley, Hammer Kearn; I'm speaking only of those who sided with the Ansons. Jerry Ryan. Nineteen dead from the shoot-out at Anson Hall. Jud lost how many deputies?"

"All but two."

"The preacher at First Baptist and Jack Miller were killed in the sheriff's department, along with old Clint and at least one other deputy. It's going to take a while to pick through the rubble."

"And it's only starting to mount up," Granger reminded the sheriff.

"Yes. We know Springer is dead, and Lucas Webster and Willie Jefferson; five or six others. Somebody ran Bugger Anson off Misty Mountain last night and made a slick spot in the road out of Eddie. Had a hell of time identifying him."

"Jane Causy and Jennifer Anson are still unaccounted for. Ralph Causy is in custody, and I put a ring of men around the Anson mansion. I thought you'd like to arrest Maxwell."

"My pleasure, sir." Son's smile was grim. "It's just incredible. I knew Maxwell and his offspring were bad . . . but Lord God, I've never heard anything like the statements we're taking. Not in twenty-five years of law work. Murder, rape, perversion, extortion, kidnapping, torture, incest, crimes against nature; the Good Lord alone knows what else. Tell me, who is this Barry Rivera fellow?"

"Oh," Granger said blandly, "some fancy-pants photographer who came in here to take pictures of old houses."

"Oh. Well, we'll save him for last . . . if we ever get around to him at all. He a fruit?"

"I didn't get that close to him to tell the truth," Granger lied. "Walked funny, though."

"I think I'll just forget I heard the name," Son said.

"Yeah, me, too."

Johnny South was packed and ready to go. He had one more little job to do. He waited on a ridge overlooking a mountain road call Hairpin, and the nickname was well deserved. Many accidents on ol' Hairpin.

Going to be another one. Erin Ramsey lived on Hairpin. Erin Ramsey bred dogs for fighting. Johnny didn't like that. Thought it a cruel thing.

Erin wouldn't be doing that again.

Johnny waited, the silencer/flash suppressor fastened to the muzzle of the rifle.

This would be Johnny's parting shot.

He chuckled at the humor and then clicked his rifle

off safety as the sound of a fast-moving vehicle reached him. Johnny caught the driver in the crosshairs. Erin.

He began humming softly. "Puff the Magic Dragon."

The fires were out, and the town, most of it, appeared normal. But the smell of gunsmoke and blood still lingered over the town in the lovely little valley.

Buses had been called in to transport the many prisoners to various jails in that part of the state.

It had done Son Cody a world of good to slap the cuffs on Sheriff Jud Manville and listen to the FBI read the bastard his rights. But Son was really looking forward—after having talked with the Wiseman girls and Goldie's sister-in-law—to popping the cuffs on Big Daddy Maxwell Anson.

One of his deputies approached Son. "Sheriff? We just come down from Willie Jefferson's house. It's a mess up there. We've got Tate Jefferson in the cage. He's the one that ain't right in the head."

"What happened?"

"We'll probably never really know. But you can scratch Jane Causy and Jennifer Anson. They're dead. Tate killed them. Then dumped their bodies over into the hog pen. You know what a hog will do to a dead body."

Son grimaced. "Did the boy say why he did that?"

"He just say they was evil."

The sheriff sighed. "Well, he was right about that."

"We fished the bodies out; what was left of them anyway. What in the world to do with Tate is what bothers me."

"Put him in a cell by himself. We'll have to have a sanity hearing."

"Yes, sir."

Another deputy said, "Sheriff? The press is hollerin' to be allowed in. Do I let them come on?"

"Not just yet. Hold them back for a few more minutes. When I put the cuffs on Maxwell Anson, let them come on in."

"Yes, sir." The deputy smiled.

"Sheriff!" a highway patrolman called. "One of our units just found Erin Ramsey. Somebody shot her right between the eyes. Long-range shooter, it looks like."

Barry was, at that time, paying his bill at the vet's office and pulling out, heading west, Dog sitting on the seat beside him. He'd been bathed and groomed.

"You look smug, Dog," Barry told him.

Dog showed him his teeth and concentrated on the passing landscape.

Barry clicked on the CB and listened to the chatter; most of it about Dane County.

"You in the Kenworth," his speaker crackled. "You come through Dane County last night?"

"10-50," Barry radioed back. "I try to avoid trouble whenever possible."

Nineteen

"Anson Inn." The familiar voice came into Barry's ear through long distance.

"How's it going, Brenda?"

She gasped her shock. "Barry?" she whispered.

"None other. Dog says hello. Things quieted down since I've been gone?"

"Where are you, Barry?"

"West Coast." That was a lie. He was in Florida. His Kenworth had been replaced with a new unit.

"I see. Well, things are returning to normal. There has been an official petition to the state to change the name of the town."

"That's good."

"Sol Wiseman and his family are preparing to move to Israel. Tate was placed in an institution. Not for punishment. Treatment. No charges against him."

"Adam?"

"No charges have been filed yet. It's all so confusing. Granger says if any charges are filed, it'll probably never come to court. A lot of old bones are being discovered as Banger and Ralph and Maxwell talk. Will I ever see you again, Barry?"

"I doubt it."

She was crying as he gently hung up the phone.

He climbed back into his rig and pulled out. "Lot of miles ahead of us, Dog. You ready for it?"

Dog was ready.

Barry's CB crackled. "You in that Kenworth . . . You got a handle?"

"Dog. Just call me Dog."